KATE KLISE

HOMESICK

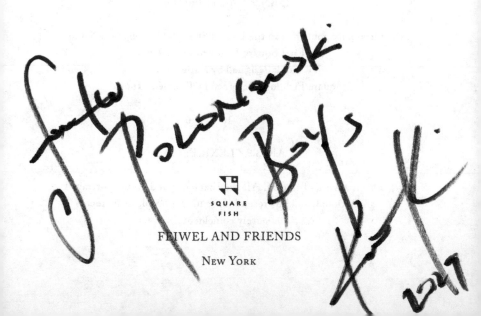

SQUARE
FISH

FEIWEL AND FRIENDS

New York

An Imprint of Macmillan
175 Fifth Avenue
New York, NY 10010
mackids.com

Square Fish and the Square Fish logo are trademarks of Macmillan and
are used by Feiwel and Friends under license from Macmillan.

Square Fish books may be purchased for business or promotional use.
For information on bulk purchases, please contact the Macmillan
Corporate and Premium Sales Department at (800) 221-7945 x5442
or by e-mail at specialmarkets@macmillan.com.

Library of Congress Cataloging-in-Publication Available

ISBN 978-1-250-06511-7

Originally published in the United States by Feiwel and Friends
First Square Fish Edition: 2014
Book designed by Katie Cline
Square Fish logo designed by Filomena Tuosto

7   9   10   8   6

AR: 3.9 / LEXILE: 610

Fifty percent of the people in the world are homesick all the time. . . . You don't really long for another country. You long for something in yourself that you don't have, or haven't been able to find.

John Cheever

See me,
feel me,
touch me,
heal me.

Pete Townshend

HOMESICK

CHAPTER 1

THE LAST SPLINTER

MY PARENTS SPLIT UP over a splinter. You've heard the expression "the last straw"? I guess this was the last splinter. The conversation went something like this:

<u>TRANSCRIPT</u>
Mom and Dad's fight: 1/20/1983

MOM (yelling): What in God's name are you doing?

DAD: Shh. You'll wake up Benny.

MOM: No, I won't. He's sound asleep.

[ME: Wrong. I was wide awake and listening from my room like I always did when my mom and dad fought. It was the soundtrack of my childhood.]

DAD: Let me just unload the truck.

MOM: I told you to clean up your crap, and now you're bringing home *more* crap?

DAD: I had to move my inventory. It wasn't safe in the store.

[ME: I should explain. Dad had a store on Highway 44 called Calvin's Collectibles. Dad said he collected treasures. Mom called it junk.]

MOM: So you're bringing all your junk *here*?

DAD: I have to protect my inventory.

MOM: Nobody wants your crap, Calvin.

DAD: My collectibles are valuable, Nola.

MOM: Oh, really? Tell me one thing you've ever owned that's valuable.

DAD: I'll tell you three things. My collection of vintage board games. My Tandy computer. And my splinter from the Holy Cross.

[ME: Ah, the mysterious splinter from the Holy Cross. I'd heard about it forever, but never seen it. Whenever I asked to see it, Dad said it wasn't a toy.]

MOM: For the love of God, don't tell me you still have the splinter of wood your grandmother gave you when you were six years old.

DAD: Think how much it's worth now.

MOM: It's worth nothing. Squat. Zero! It's a splinter, probably from your crazy granny's rocking chair.

DAD: Grammy—not granny—Grammy Summer told me it came from the Holy Crucifix.

MOM (yelling again): And you believed
her? Are you nuts, Calvin? Are you
absolutely nuts? Because you'd have to
be nuts to think you own a splinter
from the crucifix of Jesus Christ.
You're doing this to drive me crazy.

DAD: What?

MOM: That! Right there! That look on your
face. You're smirking.

DAD: I'm not smirking.

MOM: You're smirking!

[ME: He was probably smirking. Dad smirked
a lot.]

DAD: I'm thinking.

[ME: I guess he could've been thinking and
smirking.]

MOM: Uh-huh. I'm thinking, too. I'm

thinking when are you going to stop col-
lecting and start selling?

DAD: When the time's right, I'll sell
things through my computer.

MOM: What? How?

DAD: I've told you, Nola. It's coming. A
giant computer network that'll link everyone in the whole wide world. Once we're
all connected by computers, I'll be able
to sell my collection, piece by piece,
right here from the living room. I'll make
money twenty-four hours a day.

MOM: Then *sell* something already, will
you? Start with a board game. Fire up your
computer and see if anyone's buying Candy
Land tonight.

DAD: The superstructure's not ready yet.
We have to wait.

MOM: Like I haven't been *waiting* since

nineteen-stinkin'-seventy for you to
get a real job? Do you know how many motel
rooms I've cleaned since then?

DAD: Wait and watch.

MOM: Wait and watch, wait and watch,
wait and watch. No, Calvin. Stop waiting
and watch this. Where are the trash bags?
If you're bringing more junk into this
house, then I'm throwing some of your
junk out.

DAD: Don't you dare.

MOM: I have to! I can't even walk through
this house anymore without tripping over
your piles of quote-unquote collectibles.

[ME: This was true. Our house was jam-
packed with Dad's stuff, except for my
bedroom. I kept my door closed.]

DAD: I'll start cleaning tomorrow. Let me
just unload the truck now. It's late.

MOM: Are you serious?

DAD: What?

MOM: You'll really start cleaning tomorrow?

DAD: Yes.

MOM: You'll throw away some of your stuff?

DAD: Sure.

MOM: Prove it.

DAD: How?

MOM: Let me throw away one thing now. It can be something small. Tiny, even. How about that stupid splinter? I'm going to throw it away.

DAD: No. Don't. You can't.

MOM: Then *you* throw it away. Go find it. I want to see it again.

[ME: It's not a toy, Mom.]

DAD: It's not a toy, Nola.

MOM: I know. It's a sliver of wood. You showed it to me the night we met.

DAD: Mardi Gras. New Orleans. February 10, 1970.

MOM: You and your crazy splinter. It's worthless, Calvin. Throw it away.

DAD: When pigs fly.

MOM: What's that supposed to mean?

[ME: I was wondering the same thing.]

DAD: It means I'll throw away a priceless splinter from the Holy Cross on the day pigs fly.

MOM: Which means never.

DAD: I didn't say that.

MOM: You didn't have to. It's written all over your face. You're never going to get rid of anything, are you?

DAD: Never's a long time.

MOM: I'll give you one more chance. Go get your stupid splinter and throw it away.

[ME: Silence. Just the sound of Mom's furious voice hanging in the air.]

MOM: Well?

[ME: Nothing. No response from Dad. This was serious.]

MOM: Calvin, I'm asking you to choose between me and a worthless splinter.

[ME: By this point I was standing next to my door, waiting for Dad's answer.]

MOM: Fine. You've made your choice. And wow, look at that. You've managed to throw something away. Our marriage.

DAD: What about Benny?

[ME: Yeah, what about me? Don't throw me away.]

MOM: I'll come back for him when I get settled.

[ME: I could hear things rustling in the living room. Keys jingling.]

DAD: What should I tell him when he wakes up in the morning?

MOM: Tell Benny I love him and I'll be back for him soon. Oh, and tell him I signed him up for piano lessons. The first lesson is tomorrow after school. Four o'clock. Mrs. Crumple's house.

CHAPTER 2
THIS IS A TEST

I LEARNED HOW TO WRITE transcripts like that from my job at the radio station. It was a job I got because I went to my first piano lesson. Or maybe I should say because I *didn't* go to my first piano lesson.

I was standing on Mrs. Crumple's front porch on Friday afternoon, just about to knock, when I heard someone calling me from across the street.

"Benny, can you do me a favor?"

It was Myron Kazie, a floppy-haired hippie friend of Dad's who owned an electronics shop. Myron's dog, Ringo, an Australian shepherd, was at his side as usual.

"Hey, Myron," I said, relieved to have an excuse to be late for my first piano lesson. "What do you need?"

Myron wanted me to run down to the Mexican restaurant a block away, and ask Carmen, the owner, to turn her radio to 88.1 on the FM dial.

"And then what should I do?" I said.

"Just stay there and listen," Myron directed.

So I did. At first Carmen resisted.

"Radio?" she asked. "I don't know if I have one. We play cassette tapes here."

"Can you look?" I said. "It's for Myron."

"Ayyy," Carmen sighed dramatically. Two minutes later she was pulling a dusty radio off a kitchen shelf and plugging it in. I'd never been in the kitchen of Carmen's Casita. It smelled like tortilla chips mixed with Pine-Sol.

"Now what?" she asked, clearly unhappy with this chore.

"Myron wants us to turn the dial to 88.1," I said.

As soon as we did, we heard an ear-splitting noise followed by an announcement.

"This is a test. For the next sixty seconds, this station will conduct a test of the Emergency Broadcast System. This is only a test." There was a high humming sound and then we heard Myron's voice. "Benny, can you hear me? Benny? Benny? Carmen? Can you hear me down there in the restaurant?"

"What in the world?" Carmen said, staring at the radio. "Myron, can you hear me? Hello? Hello?"

"I don't think he can hear you," I said. "It's a radio, not a phone."

But Carmen wasn't listening to me. She was too busy talking to the radio. "Myron? Myron? Myron? Say something."

Two minutes later Myron was running through the kitchen door. "Did it work?" he asked, short of breath. "Could you hear me?"

"Yeah," I said. "Where were you?"

"At my new radio station," Myron replied. "KZ88, just like my name, Kazie. Isn't this great? I've always said this town needs a radio station."

"Why do we need a radio station in Dennis Acres?" Carmen asked. She was still looking at the radio like someone had pulled a trick on her.

"So you can advertise," Myron explained. "Let people know what you're cooking. Tell folks about the daily specials."

"The special's always the same," Carmen said. "Two burritos, beans, rice, chips, and salsa. Two dollars."

"I know," said Myron. "But now you can mix it up."

"Why would I want to mix it up?" Carmen demanded. Her hands were now in fists on her hips.

"Okay, so maybe you don't want to mix it up," Myron conceded. "But surely you want to hear the local news and weather."

"The weather?" Carmen said, her voice rising. "It's January. It's cold. And *news*? There's no news in a town of fifty-four people. Or fifty-three, I should say, now that Nola's left

Calvin again. But that's not news because it happens all the time, and everyone already knows it, anyway. Oh!"

Carmen looked at me and clapped her hand over her mouth.

"Benny," she said, her hand sliding down to her chin. "I'm sorry. I forget she's your mama."

"It's okay," I said.

"She'll come back," Carmen said, gently petting my cheek. "She always comes back after a day or two. You know this, yes?"

"Yeah," I lied. I wasn't sure if Mom was coming back this time or not.

"Hurricane Nola," Myron said, smiling. "That's what I call your mom. She's a hot and spicy Cajun."

"She's from New Orleans," I said. "That's how she got her name. The 'N' and the 'O' are for New Orleans. The 'L' and 'A' are for Louisiana."

"Now this I did not know," Carmen said. "See, Myron? This is something you could put on the radio. Tell us how people got their names."

I winced at the thought of anyone asking how I got my name. Nobody except my parents knew that my real name was Beignet. I was named after the deep-fried donuts Mom grew up eating in New Orleans. They're called beignets (pronounced *ben-yays*). But this was not the kind of news I was eager to have broadcast in my small town.

"I remember the first year Nola lived here," Myron was telling Carmen. "She killed a wolf spider with a shotgun. Saw it on her porch and shot it dead, just like that."

"Mom doesn't like spiders," I said. *Or messy husbands*, I thought.

Carmen was nodding her head in approval. "These are the stories you can tell on your radio station, Myron. I don't even know how Dennis Acres got its name. Tell us those things and then play music. I have some mariachi cassette tapes you can borrow."

Just then Ringo came blasting through the kitchen door. His mouth was full of tortilla chips.

"Get that dog out of my kitchen!" Carmen yelled.

"We're going, we're going," Myron said, trying to catch Ringo by the bandanna he wore instead of a collar. "Thanks for letting me test out the emergency signal. That will be a lifesaver if we ever have a hurricane or a—"

"Get OUT!" Carmen shouted as Ringo proceeded to casually jog around the kitchen, sniffing every corner and smiling. "Besides, we don't *have* hurricanes in Missouri."

"You're right," Myron said. He was having a tough time catching Ringo. "I'll concentrate on music instead. And maybe a feature on how people got their names. As you can probably guess, Ringo here got his name from—"

"I don't *care!*" Carmen hollered at the top of her lungs. "Get that dog *out* of my kitchen!"

By the time we were on the sidewalk, Myron and Ringo were both panting.

"Carmen's temper is almost as bad as your mom's," Myron said. He was retying the bandanna around Ringo's neck.

"Almost," I said.

"She'll come back," Myron added quietly.

"When pigs fly," I said.

Myron laughed. "You sound more like your dad every day. Come on, I want to show you my new radio station."

CHAPTER 3

IS THIS THING STILL ON?

THE WALK FROM CARMEN'S CASITA to Myron's shop took less than five minutes. You could walk anywhere in Dennis Acres and it wouldn't take more than five minutes. There were only three streets and twenty-nine houses in the whole town.

We passed the gas station and the post office. Next to that was the First Church of Dennis Acres, the only church in town. It was officially Baptist, but almost everyone in town attended the Sunday service, including Carmen, a Catholic, and Izzy, our Jewish postmaster. Even Myron showed up sometimes, and he claimed to be an atheist.

Myron's shop was in an old two-story white house. He lived on the second floor of the house and used the first floor for his shop. I call it a shop, which suggests people came to buy things. Not really. Most folks wanted money for broken stuff they already had: radios, TVs, electric typewriters, even vacuum cleaners.

Myron gave a dollar or two for just about anything. Then he fixed up the stuff and sold it at flea markets on the weekend. Whatever Myron couldn't fix—the "unredeemables," as he called them—he sold to my dad for five dollars a box.

"Ignore the mess," Myron said as the cowbells clanged above the front door.

He led me through the former living room and dining room to the back of the house. The place was dusty and crammed full of stuff. But unlike our house, Myron's place was organized. Radios were on one table, clock radios on another. The televisions were lined up in rows like gravestones in a crowded cemetery. Even the typewriters were displayed in a row, each machine bearing a clean white sheet of typing paper.

"This is what I wanted to show you," said Myron. He opened the kitchen door.

My first thought was: *Why would Myron hang mismatched carpet squares on the walls of his kitchen?* Cheap soundproofing, I found out later. My second thought was: *What's that big black board the size of a door with all the knobs sitting on Myron's kitchen table in the middle of the room?* A console, I found out later. It's the dashboard of a radio station. My third thought was: *Microphones and headphones. Okay, I've seen those before. And record players, too. But why would Myron need two turntables?*

So he could play songs back to back. This, too, I would learn with time.

"Cool," I said, not knowing what any of it was other than the old-fashioned school clock hanging on the wall.

"Isn't it?" Myron said. "And look at this. Alphabetical order."

He opened the kitchen cabinets. Record albums were arranged neatly inside.

"And check this out," Myron said, directing my gaze to his stove, which he'd painted bright red with the words "Hot Hits Served All Day Long."

"Cool," I repeated. "Really cool."

Myron was beaming. "How many towns our size have a radio station?"

"Not many, I bet."

"Not *any*, I'd bet," he said. "Well, I can't be certain of that. But there's no reason we shouldn't have our own station. Sure, we can get weather reports from Springfield. But they're not always accurate. And why not cover the local news? I want to do interviews with people who live right here in town."

Myron's kitchen phone rang. He answered it.

"Hello? Oh, hi, Mrs. Crumple. She what?"

Myron's eyebrows crinkled. He listened for a minute, holding the phone several inches from his ear. Then he covered the mouthpiece with his hand.

"Benny," he whispered, "do you mind waiting in the front?"

19

I left the kitchen, closing the door behind me. In the front room, I flipped on a radio and turned the dial to 88.1 FM. Mrs. Crumple was on the radio. Her voice was like a trumpet. It traveled without distortion from Myron's telephone earpiece to the microphone.

"I saw her at the gas station on Highway 71 at ten o'clock last night," Mrs. Crumple was saying. "Nola was filling her tank, which she never does. I asked where she was going that she needed all that gas. She said, 'Mrs. Crumple, I'm driving straight through to New Orleans.'"

So there it was. Mom was gone. For good.

"Said she's had it with Calvin," Mrs. Crumple continued. "Said she's never liked it here, anyway. Not the food or the coffee or the weather. But that's not all. Izzy says he won't deliver mail to the house anymore."

"Why won't Izzy deliver mail to your house anymore?" Myron asked. His voice sounded tinny coming out of the cheap radio. I moved to another table and turned on a clock radio.

"Not *my* house," Mrs. Crumple corrected sharply. "Calvin and Nola's house, only Nola's not there anymore, so it's Calvin's house. Calvin's and Benny's."

"Why?" said Myron. He sounded better on this radio. I put my head on the table and drew a circle in the dust. I moved my ear closer to the radio to hear Mrs. Crumple.

"Have you seen the house lately?" she asked. "Calvin's

always been a pack rat, but now he's filling the yard with car batteries and charcoal grills and old bikes. Izzy says last week when it snowed, he tripped on an old tricycle that was sitting right in front of their mailbox."

"I wonder why Calvin had a tricycle outside in the snow," Myron said. He was trying to sound diplomatic, like there might be a good reason why my dad, whose only child (me) was twelve years old, would have a tricycle in the front yard in the middle of winter.

"Because Calvin is a pain in the you-know-what!" Mrs. Crumple answered. "Nola works her tail off at the Diamond Inn, and Calvin doesn't even go to his shop most days. His truck isn't even *there*. He sits home on his rear end all day long. Izzy says he's considered cutting Calvin off on pizza delivery, but he didn't know what Benny would eat if he did that."

I drew a happy face in my dust circle. Whenever Mom left, Dad and I ordered pizza for dinner. It wasn't great pizza, just the frozen kind. Izzy bought it by the case in Springfield and sold it at his cost, plus two dollars for heating up and delivery.

"I'll talk to Izzy," Myron was saying. "He can deliver Calvin's mail to my shop. Benny can pick it up on his way home from school."

"That's not the point, Myron," Mrs. Crumple said.

"What's the point then, Mrs. Crumple?"

I watched the numbers on a row of clock radios turn from 4:59 to 5:00. It was like watching the odometer in the car roll over to a new hundred. Something new was in the air. A change was coming that would transform everything. Even then I could feel it, though I didn't know what it was.

"The point is," Mrs. Crumple elaborated, "Calvin's your best friend. Talk to him. Tell him to clean up his act. Either that or give him a swift kick in the pants. For Benny's sake. Speaking of whom, I'll expect to see him here next Friday afternoon for his first piano lesson."

I couldn't help myself. I jumped up from the table and ran into the kitchen, shaking my head and mouthing the words, "No, no, please no!"

Myron's eyes lit up. "Um, Mrs. Crumple? I just remembered something."

"What?" she honked.

"I'm going to need Benny's help here next Friday, so he won't be able to make that piano lesson, okay? Thanks, Mrs. Crumple."

Myron hung up the phone. Then he tapped the radio microphone.

"Is this thing still on?" he asked.

"Yeah," I answered.

"So you heard every word," Myron said. It wasn't a question.

"Yeah," I repeated. "It's okay."

Myron shook his head. "I'm sorry, Benny. I really am. But don't worry. Nobody else heard. Nobody knows about the radio station yet except you and me."

Just then Myron's phone rang again.

"Hello?" Myron said. "Oh. Hi, Carmen." He closed his eyes and frowned. "I agree, Izzy's pizza is terrible. You will? That'd be great. Thanks."

Myron hung up the phone. He turned the microphone switch on the console to the *off* position.

"Carmen's bringing dinner to your house tonight," he said. "Enchiladas."

"Cool," I said.

Myron looked at me seriously. "I don't want to give your dad a swift kick in the pants."

I laughed. "I don't, either."

Myron smiled. "But we have to do something. Your dad got behind on his rent at the store. He was evicted. Kicked out. That's why he's been moving everything from Calvin's Collectibles back home."

"Oh," I said. This was all starting to make sense.

"I've tried to convince him to hit the flea market circuit with me," Myron said, "but he won't do it. Thinks he'll get ripped off. He won't take any money from me, either. Too proud for that. I don't know what else to do."

"Get Mom to come home," I said quickly.

Myron blew out a big breath of air. "Angry women," he said, shaking his head. "Not my strong suit."

So I told Myron about the splinter.

"The alleged splinter from the Holy Cross?" he asked.

"Your dad brought that to school for show-and-tell in first grade."

"You saw it? Dad's splinter from the Holy Crucifix?"

"Well, it's a splinter all right," Myron said. "Tiny thing. Half the size of an eyelash."

"Is it real?"

"You're asking the wrong person," he replied. "I'm not much of a believer. But even if I were, a splinter almost two thousand years old?"

"It can't be real," I agreed. "He has to get rid of it. If Dad gets rid of that splinter, Mom will come home."

"But his grandmother gave it to him when he was a kid," Myron said, squinting. "He won't throw away anything his grandmother gave him. Unless . . ."

"What?"

"Unless she tells him to," Myron said.

I pointed out that both of Dad's grandmothers were dead. They died before I was born.

"I remember," Myron said. A thin grin was spreading across his face. "Benny, I think it's high time Dennis Acres had a radio séance."

CHAPTER 4

WHOA, WHOA, WHOA

IT WAS MY JOB to convince Dad to be a guest on Myron's radio show.

"But don't tell him about the séance," Myron instructed. "Just get him to bring his Ouija board when he comes for the interview."

I was at Myron's shop on Monday after school, picking up our mail. The school bus from Diamond stopped in front of Myron's shop every morning and afternoon. Our town was too small to have its own school, so the six kids in Dennis Acres went to school in Diamond, seventeen miles away.

"What's a séance again?" I asked. I still didn't get it.

"It's a game where you contact the dead," Myron said. "Or at least you pretend to."

I'd rather have been in contact with the living. My mom had been gone four days and hadn't called home yet.

"I'd talk to your dad myself, but he's ticked at me," Myron said.

"Why?"

"I cut him off," Myron said with a sigh. "I won't sell him any more unredeemables. He doesn't have the money or the space. He's mad now, but he'll get over it."

I walked home with the day's mail. Our house was just around the corner from Myron's shop. It was a one-story yellow house—or it had been yellow at one time. With all the mildew on it, our house looked more green than yellow, like the yolk of a rotten egg. The late-afternoon light didn't flatter it.

"Hey, Dad," I said, squeezing through the front door. I had to turn sideways because Dad's collectibles were stacked up in boxes next to the door. "Myron wants you to be on his radio show a week from Thursday."

"Huh?" Dad said. He was sitting on the living room floor in front of his beloved Tandy computer. He'd taken it apart and was trying to attach it to the TV, which was plopped on top of the piano bench.

"Myron wants to interview you on the radio," I said.

"Radio?" Dad asked, not looking up from his wire clippers. His hair hung in front of his stubbly face. I noticed he'd stopped shaving after Mom left.

"Myron's starting a radio station in February," I said. "He's getting everything set up now."

"Yeah," Dad mumbled. "He told me about that. Let me guess. He's going to play Led Zeppelin twenty-four hours a day."

"No," I said. "He's going to do interviews and report the news and play records. It's going to be really cool."

Dad put down his wire clippers and looked at me. "Cool? No, Benny. Radio is not cool. It's antiquated technology. What's cool is the microcomputer chip."

"Mmmokay," I said.

"Within your lifetime," Dad said, suddenly solemn, "you're going to be able to set up your own radio station on a computer. You'll be able to talk to anyone anywhere in the world."

"Can't I already do that with a telephone?"

"Sure, if you want to go broke paying long-distance charges!" Dad barked. He stood up and pointed at the tangle of wires on the floor. "This is the future, Benny. Not radio."

"Okay," I said, reminding myself of my goal. "But will you be on Myron's show? He wants to interview you about your collection of old board games. He says you should bring some games with you to talk about."

"My vintage board game collection?" Dad said, perking up. Now he was interested. "Which ones does he want to see?"

I had to be careful here. I had to sound casual. "He said you should bring Monopoly and—"

"Monopoly?" Dad interrupted. "I have a 1954 edition. In the original box."

"Okay, so take that," I said. "And Clue, Masterpiece, and, um, your Ouija board."

"Is that all?" Dad asked, making a sour face. "Those aren't even the most valuable ones."

I shrugged. "That's what Myron said he wanted. A week from Thursday. February third. Four o'clock."

"Fine," Dad said.

"I'll remind you."

"I said fine," he repeated.

I went to my room and pretended to do homework. But really I had a job to do. Myron had given me a notebook and a clock radio from his shop. My job was to listen to KZ88 and report back to him on the sound quality from our house.

I plugged in the radio. Christmas music was playing—a month after Christmas. I could hear Myron in the background. He was talking on the phone to somebody. His voice was too muffled to make out the conversation, but I made a note to remind him to use the phone in the front room rather than the kitchen phone.

Myron also wanted me to jot down some ideas for interviews. So I started making a list of people I'd like to hear on the radio.

Ideas for Radio Shows

• Mrs. Verna Hartzell. Get her to talk about why she bought a house for her cats to live in. Ask her if it had anything to do with the fact that Ringo liked to carry her cats around by the scruff of the neck and drop them wherever he pleased. (I knew Myron wouldn't take me up on this idea because Mrs. Hartzell despised Ringo, and Myron resented her for it. But it would be fun to listen to them go at it.)

• The Dennis Acres triplets: Lance, Chance, and Rance. (My dad called them the Ants brothers.) They were in my class at school. Have them describe how they counted all the sidewalk cracks (277) in town last summer. Ask if they planned to keep track of new cracks.

• Mayor Roland Prell. Get him to tell the story about how he caught a seven-foot black snake by tricking it with a white porcelain doorknob he put under his best laying hen. The snake, thinking the doorknob was an egg, swallowed it, and then got stuck trying to get out of the chicken house. Mr. Prell had been elected mayor of Dennis Acres six times by telling stories like this.

• Carmen. Have her talk about growing up in Mexico and why she moved to Missouri.

• One-armed Mr. Dallas Emery, our school bus driver. Have him talk about firecracker safety.

• Mr. Arthur Rayborn. Ask him why he always plants his garden in old tractor tires. Was it supposed to look nice? Or was it just his way of keeping rabbits out?

• Mrs. Crumple. Have her play the piano on the radio. (Possible?)

• The conductor of the Burlington Northern train. I didn't know his name or if it was even the same person every day, but it'd be interesting to hear what a train conductor thought about riding trains for a living. My dad said the train was one of the nicest things about living in Dennis Acres. Day after day, it was always there. But I guess for some people, like my mom, the train was a constant reminder that there was always some-place else you could be. Someplace better or dif-ferent or at least less messy. I wondered who I'd be when I got older: a person who heard the train rattling through town and was happy to stay? Or a person who could hear the same train and want to leave, even if it meant leaving some-thing or someone behind.

My stomach growled. I looked at the clock radio: 6:47.

"Dad?" I yelled from my bed. "Have you ordered dinner?"

"What?" he hollered back.

I slid off my bed and shuffled to the living room. "Have you ordered dinner?"

"Not yet," he said. "What do we want—sausage or pep-peroni?"

"Pepperoni," I said.

What I really wanted was Mexican food, but Dad was furious when Carmen brought over the enchiladas. He said he didn't want her or anyone's "refried pity." I knew what he really didn't want: anybody coming to our house. He wouldn't even let Izzy deliver pizza to us.

It was after eight o'clock when Dad finally walked over to Izzy's house to pick up our dinner. We ate in the living room because the kitchen stunk. The dishwasher was broken and the sink was clogged. Dirty dishes were stacked in a gray stew of water. Discarded pizza crusts floated in the water along with bloated Cheerios.

I regretted my pizza choice as soon as we finished eating. Pepperoni stunk up the house worse than sausage. I thought if I threw out the pizza box—along with the empty pizza boxes in the kitchen—it would help.

I was carrying a stack of pizza boxes to the back porch when Dad saw me.

"Whoa, whoa, whoa," he said, holding up his hands like two stop signs. "What are you doing with those?"

"I'm throwing them away," I said.

"Nope," he said, taking the boxes out of my arms. "Bad idea."

"Why?"

"Because ten years from now, there won't *be* pizza boxes like this." He was restacking the boxes in the kitchen corner. "People will get pizza from their computers. These boxes will be collectibles, trust me. We'll make a lot of money selling these to the Japanese."

"But Dad, these boxes *stink*," I said. "The whole kitchen stinks."

"Open a window if you don't like the smell," he snapped.

"Da-aad!" I could feel hot tears forming in the back of my eyes, but I forced a laugh to come out instead. "You're kidding, right, Dad?" My wobbly voice cracked on the word *Dad*.

He put the last pizza box in the corner. Then he folded his hands together as if in prayer and looked me in the eye.

"Benny, I've never been more serious about anything in my life. A worldwide computer network is coming. I've been reading about it."

"Really?" I asked in a whisper.

"Really," Dad said firmly. "It's coming and it will change everything. *Everything*. It's going to change the world. We *have* to get ready for it."

And in that moment I knew my dad had a problem—not just with pizza boxes or a holy splinter but with his whole life.

CHAPTER 5

CAREER DAY

THE KIDS FROM DENNIS ACRES who rode the school bus to Diamond were: the Ants brothers in sixth grade, Mary and Margaret Greenfield in first and third grade, respectively, and me, a sixth-grader.

A teacher also rode the bus with us. Her name was Miss Tina Turnipson. Everyone said she was the prettiest lady in town. She lived in Dennis Acres and taught kindergarten in Diamond. The Ants brothers always elbowed each other when Miss Turnipson wore short skirts to school.

In addition to her kindergarten duties, Miss Turnipson organized a weekly Career Day for sixth-graders. On Fridays, while her students were in art, Miss Turnipson came to our class (Mrs. Rosso's room) to talk about careers. Often she brought in someone to talk about a particular job. Usually it was someone's dad who milked cows or drove a truck. But on that last Friday in January, Miss Turnipson said she had a special treat for us.

"Good afternoon, sixth-graders," she began. "I'd like to introduce you all to Mr. Jack Swanson. He works for the phone company as a lineman. It's a very important job. Sometimes it can be dangerous, too."

Mr. Swanson looked like a cowboy with his tan face and leathery hands. I thought I recognized him from somewhere, but he said he didn't have kids and wasn't married. He probably mentioned those details for Miss Turnipson's benefit. He asked for her phone number and used it and the chalkboard to explain how the phone company routes calls. Then he talked about working on telephone poles, and how it wasn't all that scary once you got used to it.

As Mr. Swanson told daring stories of stringing telephone lines from pole to pole, I thought about Mom. She'd been gone a whole week now and hadn't called home once. Myron was sure we could persuade Dad to throw away the splinter during a séance. But what difference would it make if I couldn't tell Mom he'd gotten rid of it?

Mr. Swanson was talking about another job he had.

"Real estate is always a good investment," he said with his thumbs resting casually in his belt loops. "Some years I make more money off my rental properties than I do from the phone company."

That's where I recognized Mr. Jack Swanson. He was Dad's landlord. He owned the red-and-white shack Dad rented on Highway 44 for Calvin's Collectibles. I'd seen him on weekends and during the summer when I used to go with Dad to his store. It really was a shack. Years ago it had been a pancake house, but a kitchen fire destroyed the back half of the building. That's when Dad took over the lease. The whole place still smelled like charred pancakes. Mom would never spend more than ten minutes in Dad's store. She said it gave her a sick headache.

"Of course you have to have an eye for real estate," Mr. Swanson bragged. "And for people, too. The hardest part of being a property owner is when you have to evict a bad tenant. You can't let people use your property if they're not paying their rent. I had to get rid of a tenant not long ago. The guy had a store, but he wouldn't sell anything. A real nutcase, if you know what I mean."

My stomach buckled. Miss Turnipson began clearing her throat. She sounded like a sick bird with a strange cough.

"Go ahead and get some water," Mr. Swanson told her. "I can handle the kids. This is a good story." He resumed his tale. "So, this guy, this tenant of mine, got behind on his rent. I let him go for a few months. Heck, it's a tough economy. I get that. But then I started getting complaints about him. People said he was rude. Refused to sell his merchandise. I went in there one day myself and tried to buy a plastic owl.

You know, those cheapo plastic owls some people put on their house to scare away woodpeckers? Well, this guy wouldn't sell it to me. Said he couldn't let it go from his so-called collection. A plastic owl? So then I tried to buy a rusty gas can from him. But he wouldn't sell that to me, either. A gas can? Said it was more valuable than I knew."

Mr. Jack Swanson threw back his head and laughed. He was hitting full stride.

"Okay now," he said, rubbing his big hands together. "Here's a question for you future business owners. What do you do when you have a nitwit like this for a tenant? How do you get rid of loonies squatting on your property and not paying their rent?"

I felt sick with dread as I watched Mrs. Rosso, my teacher, raise her hand.

"Yeah," said Mr. Swanson, pointing at her. His fingers were positioned to look like a gun.

"I'd like to hear more about your work for the phone company," Mrs. Rosso said.

"Oh," Mr. Swanson said sadly. "I was just trying to explain how you can—"

"Excuse me, Mrs. Rosso." It was the intercom attached to the ceiling in the corner of the room.

"Yes, Mrs. Gockley?" Mrs. Rosso answered. She raised her chin and spoke directly to the intercom as if Mrs. Gockley, the school secretary, were inside it.

"Please send Benny Summer to the office," Mrs. Gockley said through the scratchy speaker.

I slunk out of class, followed by the "ooohs" and "aaaaahs" that always accompanied a request from the office. I walked down the empty hallway while the words *nitwit* and *nutcase* ricocheted in my head.

When I opened the office door, I saw Mrs. Gockley sitting at her desk. She was helping a little kid with a coat zipper.

"Your mom called, Benny," Mrs. Gockley said, struggling with the stuck zipper.

"She did?" I asked, thrilled.

"She said the phone's been disconnected at your house again."

"It has?" Even this was great news.

"She said," Mrs. Gockley continued, tugging unsuccessfully at the zipper, "you should get two twenty-dollar bills out of the coffee can in the cereal cupboard and mail the money to the phone company with your phone number and address."

"Did she say anything else?" I asked hopefully.

"No," Mrs. Gockley reported. "Just that you should pay the phone bill so she can call you." The zipper came unstuck. Mrs. Gockley smiled.

I practically floated out of the office, giddy with the knowledge that Mom had tried to call home. She'd probably tried to call home lots of times—maybe every day—thinking Dad would pay the phone bill. Why hadn't I thought to check the phone for a dial tone?

As I walked back to Mrs. Rosso's room, I tried to figure out how long it would take to get the phone turned back on if I mailed the money when I got home from school. Next Tuesday maybe? Wednesday?

I was still doing the math in my head when I returned to class. The room was quiet. My classmates were busy with a writing assignment. Mr. Swanson and Mrs. Rosso were talking softly in the back of the room. Miss Turnipson looked at me and pointed to the words on the chalkboard: *Write about an interesting job you've observed firsthand. Discuss the challenges and rewards.*

I sat down and took out my pen.

"Can I borrow a piece of paper?" I whispered to the girl behind me.

"Sure," she said, tearing a page from her notebook. She handed it to me with a smile.

Her name was Stormy Walker. She had shiny black hair and dark eyes that were long and narrow like two little feathers. She lived in a trailer house on Highway V between Dennis Acres and Diamond. Every morning, I saw her get on the school bus twenty-five minutes after me. And every afternoon, I watched her climb off the bus twenty-five minutes before me.

Of course I had notebook paper, but I liked to borrow from Stormy. It gave me an excuse to talk to her.

"Finish up your essays," Miss Turnipson instructed.

I started writing.

Being a collector is an interesting and important job. Sometimes it can be dangerous, too, because

I crumpled up my paper. Stormy laughed quietly behind me as she tore out another sheet and handed it to me. "Thanks," I whispered. I started my essay again.

Owning a collectibles store is an interesting job. You have to have an eye for valuable things. That's one of the challenges of being a collector. You have to throw away things that aren't valuable. This can be a challenge, too, because once you have something, it can start to seem valuable even if it's not.

The rewards of being a collector include the pleasure of owning lots of things and the money you make when you sell them. But you have to sell your collectibles, which can be a challenge for a collector. From my firsthand experience observing

*collectors, they are often afraid of letting go of
things. Because who knows? Something you take
for granted or think is cheap and meaningless and
seems crazy to everyone else might be really valuable someday if you can just hold on to it and find
someone who thinks it's as cool as you do.*

"All right," said Miss Turnipson. "Trade papers with the person sitting behind you."

Jeana Gockley in front of me turned around and gave me her essay. It was titled "School Secretary: Everybody's Mom."

Stormy tapped me on the shoulder. I turned around reluctantly.

"You don't have to read this," I said, handing Stormy my paper. "It's really . . . dumb."

"It can't be worse than mine," she said. "I wrote about my neighbors. They're hog farmers."

A minute later the bell rang. Miss Turnipson gathered up our essays and returned to her kindergarten class. Mr. Swanson went back to work.

"Okay, then," Mrs. Rosso said, resuming her post at the front of the classroom. "I want to see everyone stand up and do twenty jumping jacks. Then I want to see a show of hands for anyone who wants a piece of gum while we discuss the year 1789. The Bill of Rights in this country and the guillotine in

France. What a year! You're going to love it. But twenty jumping jacks first. Ready, go!"

I decided while jumping not to let my stupid essay ruin an otherwise good day.

*　*　*

When I got home from school, I paid the phone bill, according to Mom's instructions. I didn't tell Dad about it or Mom's phone message. Instead I reminded him of his upcoming interview.

"Next Thursday," I said as we ate sausage pizza in the living room. "The station's in the back of Myron's shop. He's still getting everything organized."

I was sitting on a cardboard box. Dad sat on a space he'd cleared on a corner of the sofa. The rest of the sofa was covered with magazines and unopened mail.

"Time?" Dad asked.

He was paging through a computer magazine. The TV was turned up loud, but I couldn't see it through the piles of Dad's stuff. The room was wall-to-wall junk. I looked around for the plastic owl, but didn't see it. It could've been anywhere.

"Four o'clock," I said. "Myron wants you to bring your board games. Monopoly, Clue, Masterpiece, and the Ouija board."

"Remind me later," Dad said, reading and chewing.

"I will."

I didn't mention anything about the séance or the splinter. I didn't want to jinx it. I just wanted to be able to tell Mom when she called that Dad had thrown away his holy splinter, and that she could come home now.

CHAPTER 6

GET *RIDE*?

I WAS AT MYRON'S SHOP on the afternoon of Dad's interview.

"Do you think he'll remember?" Myron asked when I arrived after school. "You might have to run home and get him."

"He'll remember," I said. I'd reminded him fifty times.

Sure enough, at ten minutes to four, the cowbells clanged as Dad walked through the door. He was carrying an armload of board games: Monopoly, Clue, Masterpiece, and the Ouija board. He also had Chutes and Ladders, Candy Land, Operation, and Battleship. He was wearing a tie over a wrinkled *Star Trek* T-shirt. I wondered if he'd forgotten this was a radio interview, not TV.

"Where do you want these?" he called.

"Calvin!" Myron answered. "Glad you could make it."

"My secretary had to rearrange my schedule a bit," Dad said.

Dad and Myron had a long-standing joke that they were busy executives with secretaries and offices and lavish expense accounts.

"I brought this, too," Dad said, pulling out a record album from under the stack of games. "Beethoven's *Greatest Hits*. Now you have some decent music to play."

"Great," Myron said, turning the album over and studying it. "Thanks, man. Now c'mon back here. I'll give you a quick tour of the station before the interview."

That took about thirty seconds. Dad just shook his head sadly.

"You put a lot of work into this," he said. "And it's all going to be obsolete when the worldwide computer network arrives. We're not going to need radio stations then, Myron. Or TV. Or even our bodies. If we want to talk, I'll just beam my hologram to you through my—"

"Dad," I said. "This is your chair right here. That's your microphone. Do you want a glass of water?"

"Sure," he said, sitting down at Myron's kitchen table. For a minute he looked almost nervous. He reached under the table and gave Ringo a scratch behind the ears.

I poured water for Dad and Myron and set the glasses on the table.

"I'm going to be sitting across from you like this," Myron said to Dad. "Benny, get your notebook because I want you to make a transcript of this interview."

"A what?" I asked.

"Write down everything we say," Myron instructed. "I want to keep transcripts from all my interviews. For historical purposes."

At four o'clock on the dot, Myron dropped the needle on a *Sesame Street* record and played the opening bars of "People in Your Neighborhood." Then he used the levels on the console to fade the music out and bring his microphone up.

"Welcome to 'The People in Your Neighborhood,'" Myron said in his best radio announcer voice. "This is the show that lets you learn a little bit more about the people in *our* neighborhood, the little place that time forgot that we call Dennis Acres, Missouri."

Myron paused to cough quietly into his hand. He took a sip of water. Maybe he was nervous, too.

"For my first interview," he continued, "I couldn't be happier to have my best friend, Calvin Summer. Thanks for being here, Cal."

"A pleasure," Dad said, leaning into his microphone.

They looked like a hippie comedy team: Dad, the stockier of the two, with his scruffy beard and greasy hair, sitting across from skinny Myron, with his wire-rim granny glasses and Led Zeppelin T-shirt.

But Dad sounded good. His voice was rich and deep. If anyone was driving through Dennis Acres just then and happened to turn the radio dial to 88.1 FM, they might think Dad was a hotshot businessman in a three-piece suit instead of a guy in dirty jeans who collected old board games.

"Calvin and I go way back," Myron was saying. "We went to school together over in Diamond. Class of '69. Played baseball. You pitched. I was the home-run kid. We thought we were going to play for the St. Louis Cardinals, remember?"

"You were the best man at my wedding," Dad said.

"That's right," Myron said. "I was."

"Yep," Dad said. "And for anyone who's listening and wondering about Nola, she left a couple weeks ago. She got mad about my holy splinter."

Myron blinked. He hadn't planned on getting to the splinter so soon in the interview.

"Your holy splinter?" Myron asked, rubbing his chin. "Didn't you bring that to show-and-tell in first grade? Your Grammy Summer gave it to you, right? Was she the one who could catch mice with her bare hands?"

"That's her," Dad replied. "She gave me the holy splinter when I was six. Told me it was given to her by her grandfather, who got it from his grandfather, who got it from someone who knew for a fact that it was a splinter from the cross of Jesus Christ."

"Uh-huh," Myron said.

47

"Nola wanted me to get rid of it," said Dad, crossing his arms.

"And you said?" Myron asked.

"When pigs fly."

"Riiiiight," said Myron, nodding his head. "Right."

A few seconds of silence followed, which I was grateful for. As fast as I was writing, I was having a heck of a time keeping up with this conversation.

"Folks, that's just one of the many interesting stories Calvin Summer could tell," Myron said. "And I see you've brought some games with you, Calvin. Tell us what you have here."

Dad launched into a fifteen-minute lecture on the history of board games, the value of vintage pop culture collectibles, and the importance of keeping games in their original boxes.

"And a Ouija board," Myron said, acting surprised to see it. "Mind if I take this one out of the box?"

"Not if you're careful," Dad answered.

"This brings back memories," Myron said. "Remember the nights we tried to rouse the ghost of Abraham Lincoln?"

"Yeah. And Jesse James, too," Dad recalled. "We wanted to know where he buried all his money."

Myron laughed. "We should try to contact someone right now. Why not? We've got some time to kill."

Dad was hesitant, but Myron convinced him. I turned off

all the lights in the kitchen except for one desk lamp so I could see to write.

"Okay then," said Myron. "Who should we contact? Oh, I know. How about Grammy Summer?"

"I'm not sure that's a good—" Dad started to say.

"It'll be fun!" Myron jumped in. "She'll be tickled to hear from us. Now folks, for those of you at home who don't know how a Ouija board works, let me explain. We have a board here with every letter of the alphabet. We'll ask Calvin's dead grammy a question, and then her spirit will guide our fingers to spell out the answer. Are you ready?"

"I guess," Dad said.

Myron told me earlier how it really worked. He would push the little plastic game piece to the letters to spell out the answers he wanted.

"Okay," said Myron. "Go ahead, Calvin. Close your eyes and ask a question."

"Grammy Summer," Dad said slowly, with his eyes closed. "Can you hear me?"

"Y," Myron said.

"E," Dad said, opening his eyes.

"S," Myron said. "Yes! She can hear us. Ask another question, Calvin."

"Let's see," Dad said. "Grammy Summer, do you like my necktie?"

"Y," Myron said.

"E," Dad said.

"S," Myron said. "Yes! She likes your necktie. My turn now." He lowered his voice and spoke in a slow, deep growl. "Grammy Summer, if you can hear me, tell us what Calvin should do with the holy splinter you gave him."

Dad looked at him hard. "It's not a toy, Myron."

I had to bite the inside of my mouth to keep from laughing.

"I know it's not a toy," Myron replied gravely. "But I'm curious to hear what Grammy Summer has to say about it after all these years."

Myron and Dad placed their fingers solemnly on the plastic game piece.

"G," Myron said softly.

"E," Dad added seriously.

"T," Myron said louder.

"R," Dad said faster.

"I," Myron said excitedly.

"D?" Dad asked.

"Get rid," Myron said mysteriously. "Oh! Get *rid* of it!"

"Wait," said Dad. "She's adding another letter. E."

"Get ride?" Myron asked.

"Get ride," Dad repeated. "I knew it. I've been thinking about building a motorcycle out of scrap parts. Now I know Grammy Summer wants me to do it. Get *ride*. Get it? She wants me to get a motorcycle to ride."

"I didn't feel that last 'E' at all," Myron said feebly. "We were asking about the splinter. I'm pretty sure she said get *rid* of it."

"Nope, nope, nope," Dad said, shaking his head. "I'm positive it's about a motorcycle. Remember how Grammy Summer wouldn't let us ride motorcycles when we were kids? Said they were too dangerous?"

"Kinda," Myron conceded in despair.

"Well, now Grammy's telling me it's okay," Dad explained. "Wow. I wasn't sure if I should build one or not. But if Grammy Summer wants me to, then I *have* to do it."

Ringo began moaning mournfully under the table.

Dad pointed to the dog. "See? Ringo's picking up on the same message. He's trying to make the sound of a motorcycle. Benny, be sure you get what Ringo's saying in the transcript."

"Okay," I said.

Dad gathered up his board games. He pushed back his chair and stood up.

"Thanks, Myron," he said. "I've really enjoyed this. Man, for years I thought Grammy Summer was mad at me."

"Why would Grammy Summer be mad at you?" Myron asked in a defeated voice, his hands now rubbing his forehead.

Dad looked around suspiciously. "I wasn't supposed to take the holy splinter out of the house," he whispered. "It's priceless, you know. But she must not be mad at me if she says I can build a motorcycle. How do you like that? Wish I could stay longer, but I've got to go to the scrap yard to look for parts." He stopped and looked at me. "Aren't you supposed to be at your piano lesson?"

"Uh," I said. "That's another day."

* * *

Dad and I had pepperoni pizza for dinner that night. The stack of boxes in the kitchen was growing.

"Pretty soon we'll have ourselves the leaning tower of pizza boxes," Dad said with a laugh. The séance had put him in a banner mood. "Whaddya think of that? The leaning tower of pizza? That's pretty good, huh?"

"Not bad," I said. We were eating in the living room, but the smell of ripening garbage from the kitchen was already creeping through the house. The sickening smell clung to every wall. I always kept my door closed with a towel stuffed under the bottom to keep the stink out. It was my way of keeping Dad out, too, since my door didn't have a lock.

Dad was in the bathroom when Mom called later that night. I pulled the phone into my bedroom and closed the door.

"Mom," I said softly, stuffing the towel back under the door. "Hi!"

"Hey, sweet dreams," she said. "You didn't think I forgot about you, did you?"

"No," I said. Though come to think of it, I sort of did.

But hearing her call me "sweet dreams" changed everything. How could an expression I thought I loathed suddenly make everything better? I felt my body relax for the first time in weeks. *Everything is going to be fine,* I thought.

"I paid the phone bill," I said.

"I know," she said. "That's why I can finally call."

"Where are you?" It sounded like she was standing in the middle of a highway.

"A phone booth," she answered. "Louisiana."

"Oh," I said.

It sounded so far away.

"Here's the plan," Mom said. "You're going to stay in Dennis Acres until the end of the school year. That's just the rest of February, March, April, and part of May. Then I'm going to come get you and bring you back here."

"Where?"

"New Orleans. Well, just across the river from New Orleans. It's a town called Gretna. I've got a cleaning job at a motel. You'll go to school here next year."

"What about Dad?"

"He'll stay there," she said. "He likes it there."

"But," I said.

"But what?" Her voice was hard.

But who will take care of him?

"It's going to be fine, Benny," she said. "I can't wait to take you to Café du Monde in New Orleans for beignets.

You'll love 'em. Little fried donuts covered in powdered sugar. Mmm!" She smacked her lips together. "Sweet treats for my sweet dreams."

"But," I said again.

The "sweet dreams" magic was gone. The spell had been broken.

"It's late," she said. "I'm almost out of change. We'll talk another time."

I wanted to tell her how Myron and I had tried to get Dad to throw away the splinter. But that would just make her mad. I wanted to ask if she felt homesick. But I already knew the answer to that. I wanted to say that *I* felt homesick. But I hadn't even left home. How could I be homesick?

"Dad's going to build a motorcycle," I said quickly.

"What?" Mom demanded. "How's he going to buy a motorcycle?"

"Not buy. Build."

"He's going to build a motorcycle?" she asked. "Out of what?"

"Stuff," I said. *Junk,* I thought.

"Don't get on anything he builds," Mom ordered. "I mean it, Benny. It's not safe. Do you hear me?"

"Yeah."

"Has he cleaned the house yet?" she asked.

I didn't know what to say.

"I bet he hasn't," Mom said. Her words were clipped. "Talk fast, Benny. I'm almost out of coins. Has he thrown anything away?"

"Not really," I said. "Not yet."

"I knew it. I'll call again when I can. Bye."

The line went dead.

She wasn't coming home. It didn't matter whether Dad got rid of the splinter or not. She was never coming back, except to get me and take me to Louisiana.

I couldn't fall sleep that night for the longest time. When I finally did, I dreamed of a giant Ouija board. I was a little Monopoly piece. Something big and strong kept blowing me across the board and screaming, "I'm asking you to choose between a donut, a motorcycle, and a splinter. Make your choice!"

I didn't like it, but I couldn't make the dream stop. I kept moving from letter to letter, spelling the same sad words: G-E-T-R-I-D-O-F. There was one more word with three letters. It was blurry, but I knew what the word was. I knew who I was supposed to get rid of. And it killed me inside just to think of getting rid of him.

CHAPTER 7

TURN IT UP WITH TINA TURNIPSON

MYRON SAID HE LIKED MY IDEAS, but he never interviewed the people I suggested. Instead, he started a new show on Tuesday afternoons called "Turn It Up with Tina Turnipson."

On the day of her first interview, Miss Turnipson sat next to me on the bus after school. She held a large shopping bag on her lap.

"I hear you're working at the radio station," she said. "Mr. Kazie told me you've been *very* helpful."

"'Sbetter than taking piano lessons," I mumbled. The Ants brothers were sitting three rows ahead. They were turned around in their seats, laughing and making kissy faces. Lance was winking and giving me the thumbs-up.

"Gosh, I hope I do okay," Miss Turnipson said. "I've never been on the radio before."

"You'll do fine," I said. I was staring right back at those stupid Ants brothers and making gestures with my chin for them to turn around and mind their own beeswax.

"Is a fly bothering you, Benny?" Miss Turnipson asked. "It seems early for insects."

"No, it's just . . . I'm . . . nothing," I said, trying to ignore the Ants brothers.

"That's good," she replied. "Golly, I hate flies. Once a fly flew in my ear like this and . . . Oh, darn it all!"

She dropped the bag from her lap. Plastic beads and colorful masks spilled all over the floor of the bus. I crawled under my seat and started gathering up her things.

"Thank you, Benny," Miss Turnipson said as I passed her handfuls of spaghetti-like plastic necklaces. "Did you know today's Mardi Gras? I always bring in my collection of beads and doubloons for the kiddos to play with. We had a parade at recess. Did you see us?"

"No," I said. I was still crawling around on the grimy bus floor. I was trying to reach a red painted mask that was wedged under the seat in front of me. I could hear the Ants brothers dying of laughter.

"Oh, that's great," Miss Turnipson said when I handed her the red mask. She stuffed it in her bag. "That's my favorite mask. He looks like a smiling cannibal, doesn't he? Or some kind of savage, maybe? Supposed to scare off demons. It's hand-carved wood."

"I noticed," I said, sliding back into my seat. I got a dang splinter in my finger from the stupid mask.

"You know what Mardi Gras is, don't you, Benny?" Miss Turnipson asked. "It's the day before Ash Wednesday. Some people call it Fat Tuesday because they pig out before Lent begins. Are you giving up anything for Lent?"

I've already given up my mom, I thought. *Am I really expected to give up something else?*

"I don't believe in giving up things for Lent," Miss Turnipson continued, carrying on a lively conversation all by herself. "It's a little pagan for my tastes. I leave that to the Catholics. Wasn't your mom Catholic?"

She's not dead, I thought. *She's just gone.*

A half hour later, Miss Turnipson was sitting in front of a microphone across the table from Myron. He had a red bandanna twist-tied around his head. This was about as dressed up as Myron ever got.

"Tina Turnipson," Myron began. "Tell us something about yourself we don't already know."

"Well, Mr. Kazie, one thing you might not know about me is that I'm taking a creative writing class at the community college in Joplin."

"You are?" Myron marveled. "That sounds interesting."

No, it didn't. Hearing about a black snake that swallowed a doorknob would've been ten times more interesting.

"Tell us all about creative writing," Myron said grandly, like he was a prince asking Cinderella to dance.

Jeez Louise. Myron was worse than Mr. Jack Swanson. If he wanted to spend time with Miss Tina Turnipson, why didn't he just ask her out on a date? I knew why. Because she'd say no. I cursed the day I agreed to write transcripts for Myron.

Truth is, I was grouchy because I was out of clean clothes and I didn't know how to do laundry. I'd been washing my shirts and underwear in the bathroom sink. Nothing ever got completely clean. Even worse, nothing ever got completely dry. I felt like a wet mutt in my damp clothes. I hoped like heck Stormy Walker didn't notice.

That's another reason I was grouchy. Here it was the day after Valentine's Day and I hadn't mustered the nerve to give Stormy a Valentine. She was the only girl I'd ever liked. Why hadn't I given her something?

As Miss Turnipson prattled on about the joys of creative writing, I wondered where Stormy got her name. It sounded to me like an Indian name. Maybe she had family in a tribe. Dennis Acres wasn't far from the Oklahoma border, and there were lots of tribes across the state line. But I was too shy to ask Stormy about her name, let alone give her a Valentine.

Whoops. I was missing whole paragraphs of the interview.

When I started paying attention again, Miss Turnipson was talking about a contest.

"They want to find the most charming small town in America," she was saying. "So I wrote an essay and did a little pen-and-ink rendering of Dennis Acres. See?" She handed Myron a drawing.

Myron looked at it closely. "This being radio and all, I better explain what we have here so folks at home can see it in their minds. Well, it's a pretty little picture, I'll say that for starters."

"Thank you," said Miss Turnipson sweetly.

"I like these cottages here with the thatched roofs and the gardens in front," Myron continued. "And the little curls of smoke coming out of the chimneys. There's a nice town square with a fountain in the middle. Heck, I'd like to live here."

Miss Turnipson giggled. "I took a few liberties with our village."

Myron looked confused. His eyes went from the drawing to Miss Turnipson and back again. "This isn't supposed to be a picture of Dennis Acres, is it?"

"It's a *rendering*," Miss Turnipson said as if she were correcting a slow kindergartner. "It's my, well, personal interpretation of where we live."

"Oh," Myron said. "Is that allowed in the contest? I mean, I don't see my shop in this picture or Carmen's Casita or, um . . ." Myron looked at me. I knew what he was thinking:

I don't see Calvin Summer's trash heap of a house in this picture, either.

"I didn't draw absolutely every little thing," Miss Turnipson explained with dewy eyes. "I wanted Dennis Acres to look charming." She picked a long brown hair off the kitchen table and flicked it onto the floor. She looked upset. I hoped she wasn't going to cry.

"Oh, I get it," said Myron gently, tilting his head. "Because that's the contest, right? America's Most Charming Small Town."

"Yes," said Miss Turnipson, stifling a sniffle. "Exactly."

"Is there a prize?" Myron wondered aloud.

"There is," said Miss Turnipson, brightening. "The U.S. Chamber of Commerce is going to send representatives from Washington, D.C., to the winning town to set up computers in everyone's homes. Then they'll connect them all together with wires. Or maybe rope or yarn. I don't really understand it all. It's something about connecting everyone in town and eventually everyone in the world with one big computer."

I stopped writing. "The worldwide computer network?" I asked.

"Something like that," she answered stiffly. "As I said, I don't know all the details. I just know whatever town wins will be the first town in America connected with one big computer nougat. No, that's not it. What's it called again?"

"A network," I whispered. My brain was whirling. Maybe Dad was right. *Could Dad possibly be right?*

"I've heard of this," Myron said. "My friend Calvin is all over this stuff. But somebody tell me, why do we need a big computer to connect us all together?"

"Oh, it's going to be a wonderful educational tool," Miss Turnipson professed. "With this giant computer nougat, children will be able to ask a question—any question at all—and the computer will spit out an answer." She snapped her fingers. "Just like that. And once we connect all the computers together with extension cords, we'll have even more power, so we can ask more questions. Harder questions, too."

"Is this giant computer going to be able to tell me where I left my glasses?" Myron asked. "Or when I'm going to have a flat tire? 'Cause that would be handy."

"Now that I don't know," said Miss Turnipson seriously. "It's possible."

"Is this computer going to do away with radio?" Myron asked.

"I'm not an expert, Mr. Kazie," Miss Turnipson replied.

"Well, I *am* an expert in radio," said Myron, his tone suddenly harsh.

(Wow, this was getting good! I was glad I stuck around.)

"Or at least I feel like I'm becoming an enlightened amateur," Myron said, backpedaling a bit. "I'm learning new things every day. And that's the thing about radio. Sure, it's low-tech. It's cheap and easy. Anyone can do this stuff. But radio forces your mind to make up the picture. It exercises your brain. People listening to us right now have to imagine what we look like. Maybe they're wondering what you're wearing, and if I'm getting hot and sweaty having to defend my little radio station here against this worldwide giant computer net that's going to come swoop down and trap me and everyone else under it."

He paused to take a sip of water. Miss Turnipson bit her lower lip.

"Sorry if I got a little wound up there," Myron said.

"It's okay," Miss Turnipson said. "And the truth is, we don't have a snowball's chance in you-know-where of winning this contest."

"We don't?" asked Myron, smiling.

"No," admitted Miss Turnipson. "It's just an assignment in my creative writing class."

"Well, in that case I'm all for entering," Myron said, beaming. "Draw pictures of little angels dancing around Dennis Acres. Tell the judges even our raccoons are polite. Yessiree, the raccoons here are so polite, they put the lids back on the garbage cans when they're done eating."

Miss Turnipson laughed. "I've already written my essay. I just have to mail it."

After the interview, I walked with Miss Turnipson as far as my house.

"I have to stop by the post office to buy stamps for the application," she said. "Let's cross fingers for triple luck."

"Do what?" I asked.

"Watch," she said, crossing her fingers. "Now you cross your fingers, too, and then we'll cross them over the envelope together. Three crosses. It's triple lucky."

I curled my middle finger over my index finger, which was already sore because of the dang splinter. Then I held my crossed fingers over Miss Turnipson's crossed fingers. It was the closest thing I'd ever done to holding hands with a girl. And shoot, Miss Turnipson was pretty. There was no denying it. Wouldn't the Ants brothers just die if they could see me now? And Mr. Jack Swanson, too.

The envelope addressed to "America's Most Charming Small Town Contest" went out in the next morning's mail. The future of Dennis Acres was forever changed.

CHAPTER 8

SERVICE WITH A SMILE

TWO WEEKS LATER AT SCHOOL, Mrs. Rosso gave us an assignment.

"As you know," she began, "sixth-graders are expected to complete a volunteer service project during the second semester of school."

This news was met with the expected collective groan.

"No, no, no," she said, waving two fingers like windshield wipers. "I don't want to hear complaints. Because if you complain, it's not voluntary service."

If we have to do it, I thought, *there's nothing voluntary about it.*

"Service should be delivered with a smile," Mrs. Rosso said, smiling. "You don't want the person you're helping to feel sorry for you. On the contrary, you want the person to think you're enjoying the privilege of being allowed to help."

"That isn't service," I whispered to Stormy over my shoulder. "That's acting."

She laughed quietly behind me. One good thing about spending time with Miss Turnipson during her Tuesday afternoon interviews was that it was bolstering my courage around Stormy.

"Now," Mrs. Rosso explained, "as part of this project, Deputy Rodney will visit our class tomorrow to talk about the various places you can volunteer. Give it some thought. Find a cause you believe in. You'll also be writing a report about your service project."

Oh, the groans that followed! Mrs. Rosso just closed her eyes and grinned. She'd been teaching sixth grade long enough to know we didn't blame her. Truth is, we all liked Mrs. Rosso. Not only did she play kickball with our class during recess, she also gave out full-size Snickers to kids who went trick-or-treating to her house in Diamond. It was one of the reasons everyone liked Mrs. Rosso—that and the old claw-foot bathtub filled with pillows in the back of her classroom. We got to take turns reading in the tub during silent reading time. It was just a silly thing, but when it was your turn to read in the tub you couldn't help but feel cool.

Deputy Rodney was decidedly less cool. He sounded like a zombie as he ticked off the various places we could volunteer.

"You could pick up trash along a road or highway," he suggested in a monotone. "You could read to senior citizens in a retirement home. You could deliver mail to patients at the hospital. You could clean gutters at the jail. You could volunteer as a pet groomer at the county animal shelter."

This last idea prompted several shouts of "Mine!" "I get to do that!" and "I said it first!"

"Please remember," Mrs. Rosso said, holding up a hand, "that you're responsible for getting yourself to and from your service project. I don't want you asking your parents for rides because then it's not fully *your* project."

I could hear Stormy let out a sigh behind me. The county animal shelter was in Neosho, probably twenty minutes from Stormy's trailer. Way too far to get to on a bike.

"What're you going to do for your project?" I asked Stormy later that afternoon as we were waiting for the bus. I'd learned from watching Myron that the easiest way to start a conversation with a girl you liked was by asking a question.

"Service project?" Stormy replied. "I don't know. What I'd really like to do is help my mom find a job. Maybe look through the phone book and find businesses and addresses, and then type some letters for her? I don't know if that'd count. I'm not sure we can do service stuff for our own family."

"I bet Mrs. Rosso will let you," I said. "What kind of work does your mom do?"

"She used to cook in a hospital cafeteria," said Stormy.

"But she kept missing work because of our car. It doesn't always run. So she lost her job. But she can't fix the car until she gets money from another job. And she can't get another job until she fixes the car."

"What about your dad?" I asked.

"He's not really . . . around," Stormy said.

A million thoughts flew through my head. *Should I tell her about my mom leaving? Should I tell her about my dad's lack of employment? Did she already know about Dad from reading my Career Day essay? Were her parents divorced? Did her dad visit or call her?*

Before I could decide which question to ask, the bus arrived. As usual, Stormy sat in the front row and I sat near the back. She threw up once on the bus and had sat in the front ever since. It helped her stomach, she said, if she could see the road. A lot of kids got sick on Highway V. They're the ones who said it was named Highway V because it made you vomit. But the hilly road never bothered me. I liked the country roller-coaster ride between home and school.

The next day I heard Stormy talking to Mrs. Rosso about her service project idea.

"Perfect," Mrs. Rosso declared. "That's exactly what you should do, Stormy. I'll show you how to make a résumé for your mom. This'll be fun."

Stormy smiled at me as she walked back to her desk.

"I told you she'd let you," I whispered.

"I wasn't sure," she whispered back.

"There's a restaurant in Dennis Acres that might need a cook," I whispered, hungry to keep the conversation alive. "It's called Carmen's Casita."

"I've been there," Stormy said softly. She was writing it down. "That's a good idea. Thanks!"

"You're welcome," I said. "Anytime!"

I still didn't have an idea for my project. After the last bell rang, I stayed behind in Mrs. Rosso's room. She was arranging the pillows in the bathtub.

"Mrs. Rosso?" I said. "Can I do a service project at my house, like Stormy's doing?"

"Tell me your idea," she said.

"Well," I began. "Um, uh . . ."

I immediately regretted launching this conversation. How could I possibly explain the situation at home?

"Yes?" Mrs. Rosso said. She was flipping the pillows over and fluffing them up with the palms of her hands.

I took a deep breath and started talking fast. "See, my mom's been on a trip to Louisiana, and my dad and I are both kinda, um, messy, I guess you could say."

Why was I telling Mrs. Rosso this? Or did she already know? Did everybody know?

"What are you thinking, Benny?" Mrs. Rosso said gently.

"Just that, um, maybe I could try to clean up around the house? I mean, the kitchen is a disaster. It's, like, a real wreck."

I pretended to laugh. "The living room, too. But I could clean up some of the other rooms. Maybe start in my room and go from there? If I could figure out how to work the washer and dryer, I could wash some clothes for my dad and me. I think we have a box of Tide somewhere."

Mrs. Rosso stopped fluffing pillows. She was staring at me. Her face looked dead serious.

"Benny," she said, "don't you dare tell anybody I said this, but that's the best idea I've heard all day."

"Really?"

"Really. Do it and then write about it. You're a strong writer, Benny. I can see you writing books when you get older. That's a career you should consider. Oh, and here, let me write down a really easy way to do laundry."

When I got off the bus that afternoon, I didn't linger at the radio station like I usually did. I stayed just long enough to pick up our mail and say hi to Myron. He was crouched under the console with a jumble of phone lines.

"I'm trying to rig up a system where people can call into the station," he said when I asked what he was doing. "I want to have audience participation on our interview shows."

"Do a whole show where people call in and tell snake stories," I suggested. "Everyone has a good snake story. Did you know the Ants brothers got chased by a hoop snake last summer? The snake got mad and rolled itself into a hoop by putting its tail in its mouth. Then it chased them around their yard for hours."

"Rural legend," Myron said from under the table. "There's no such thing as a hoop snake, even though boys like you have been telling stories about them for years."

"Really?" I said. "But the snake-swallowing-the-doorknob story is true. Mr. Prell doesn't lie. He's the mayor."

"Mmm," Myron mumbled. "I wonder if your dad would help me run these phone lines. Doesn't have to be today."

"I'll ask him. I'm going home now."

"Thanks," said Myron. He poked his head out from under the table and rubbed his eyes. "Did you know your dad was the smartest kid in our class?"

"He was?"

"Yeah. He didn't always get the best grades, but he was head and shoulders above the rest of us. Smartest kid in the whole school, in fact."

I found that hard to believe.

"That's why it's such a shame," said Myron, crawling back under the console table. "A crying shame."

* * *

Dad was sitting in the living room. He was surrounded by a pile of greasy motorcycle parts he'd found at the scrap yard. He was eating popcorn. He'd recently found a movie theater–style popcorn maker, also at the scrap yard. The word "Cornucopia" was written in dancing popcorn kernels across the front. Dad claimed the machine was brand new. We'd been making popcorn almost every night for dinner. I was sick of it after two nights, but the smell was better than pizza. And no stinky boxes, either. The stack of empty pizza boxes in the kitchen had grown almost as tall as me.

"Hey, Dad," I said. "Myron wants to know if you'll help him run some phone lines."

"Mmm?" Dad said. He was chewing a mouthful of popcorn and looking at an engine diagram in an old *Encyclopedia Britannica.*

"Myron needs help," I said. "At the radio station. Doesn't have to be today."

"The radio station, eh?" said Dad, not looking up. He never listened to the radio. He preferred game shows on TV.

"Yeah. Will you help him run some phone lines? He wants to be able to take calls when he's on the radio."

"The radio," Dad repeated absently, scratching his beard with a screwdriver. "What's his station called? Crazy eighty-eight?"

"KZ88," I said. "It's 88.1."

"Right," Dad said. "Idiot point one."

I couldn't listen to him anymore. I went to my room and closed the door. Then I started to clean.

I grabbed a pile of clothes off the floor and walked the bundle to the laundry room. I dumped my jeans and dark shirts in the washing machine along with a cup of Tide, as Mrs. Rosso had instructed. My clothes were so stinky, though, I added another cup of detergent, just to be sure. I turned the first knob to *heavy load* and the second knob to *cold*. I pulled the *ON* knob out. The machine started filling up with water. That was easy.

I poured another cup of Tide in my hand and carried it to my bathroom. I poured some of the detergent in my sink, some in the tub, and the rest the toilet. I found a toilet brush in the cabinet under the sink and used it to scrub everything. I rinsed the sink and tub with hot water and flushed the toilet twice.

I returned to my bedroom and gathered up another load of dirty clothes. I dumped that pile in front of the washing machine. I made four piles in all.

Next, I went to the kitchen and found a box of garbage bags under the sink. The smell in the kitchen was lethal. I knew I couldn't tackle that room. So I went back to my room and started filling a garbage bag with old school papers, candy wrappers, Kleenex, and old Matchbox cars I hadn't played with since third grade.

My bedroom looked noticeably better after only ten minutes. I ripped the already torn *Star Wars* poster off my wall and stuffed it in the bag. Ditto the empty bulletin board my mom had insisted I'd like. (I didn't.) I pulled the sheets off my bed and wadded them up in a pile along with the empty pillow-cases and several towels. I'd wash those in hot water next.

Now that I could see the floor, I decided to vacuum. I had no idea where the vacuum cleaner was.

I looked in the hall pantry. It smelled liked cat urine. We hadn't had a cat since I was in first grade.

I tried Mom and Dad's room. The bed was piled high with computer equipment. Dad had been sleeping on the living-room couch ever since Mom left. All of his clothes were on the bedroom floor. I opened the closet. Dad had filled it with empty unwashed jars. The hideous smell of rotting mayonnaise and salad dressing made me gag.

I looked in Mom and Dad's bathroom. Dozens of empty toilet paper rolls were piled in a corner. I pulled my T-shirt out so it formed a bowl and loaded it with the cardboard rolls, which I carried to my bedroom and dropped in the garbage bag.

"Dad," I yelled from my room. "Where's the vacuum cleaner?"

"The what?" he yelled back.

I walked to the living room. "The vacuum cleaner," I repeated.

"What do you need that for?"

"I'm cleaning up around here."

"Why?" he asked.

"Because this place is a dump," I said. "And I'm sick of it."

"Sorry to hear that," he said casually. He was still looking at the encyclopedia.

I crossed my arms. "Did you know everyone in Dennis Acres might win a computer?"

This was my magic bullet. I hadn't told him about the contest. I'm not sure why. I guess I liked knowing something he didn't know. I felt important delivering the news.

"I think we have a pretty good shot at winning," I added, even though I knew it wasn't true.

"No, we don't," Dad answered without lifting his eyes.

"How do you know?" I said.

"Myron told me all about it. Dennis Acres—America's Most Charming Small Town?" He laughed cynically. "There's a good one."

I don't think I've ever been as mad at anyone as I was right then.

Dad must've noticed. "Relax," he said, "I'm going to help Myron with his phones."

"You are?"

" 'Course," he said. "He's my best friend. I always help him. Poor Myron's had a rough ride."

"What do you mean?"

"For one thing, his girlfriend died on graduation night," Dad said. "Myron was driving. He walked away without a scratch. She was D.O.A."

"What?"

"Dead on arrival," Dad said.

I swallowed hard. "I never knew that."

"Lotta things you don't know."

"I guess." I started to walk out of the living room.

"Where are you going?" Dad asked.

"I told you. I'm looking for the vacuum cleaner."

"Why?"

"Because I'm cleaning the dang house."

"Why?"

"Because I *want* to!" I said. "And because I have to. For school. We have to do a service project, and this is mine."

Dad looked at me hard. "You have to clean our house for school?"

I sighed. "Every sixth-grader has to do a service project. It's a school tradition. Mrs. Rosso said for my project I could clean our house."

"Rosso?" Dad said. He was getting up. He was digging through one of his piles.

"Yeah, Mrs. Rosso. She's my teacher."

Dad found a telephone book. He was paging through it.

"Rosso, Rosso," he said. "Does she live in Diamond?"

"Yeah, I think so. Why?"

"There's only one Rosso listed," he said. He found the phone under a stack of books and dialed.

"Hello?" he said into the phone. "Calvin Summer here.

I'm looking for a Mrs. Rosso who teaches sixth grade at Diamond School. It is? Good. Because I want to know what you think you're doing making my son clean our house for a school project. Uh-huh. Are you planning to pay him for this work? I see. And are you familiar with child labor laws? Right. Uh-huh. That's very interesting because are you aware, Mrs. Rosso, that that's not what school is for? Your job is not to teach my son how to clean houses. Your job is to teach him history and math. And do you know what I've noticed, Mrs. Rosso? You're not doing a very good job."

"Dad!" I gasped, horrified.

"No, let me finish," Dad said, waving me away. "Your job is to teach my son how to think, Mrs. Rosso. How to think. *Think!*"

"Dad," I said again, shaking my head frantically.

"Is that so, Mrs. Rosso?" Dad was saying. "The 'Mrs.' in your name suggests there's a Mr. Rosso. Do you assign him asinine service projects like you do your students? Do you treat him like a child, too?"

"Dad!" I shouted.

"I'm just asking," Dad said, trying to sound innocent. He had his back to me now. "I'm just wondering because I don't think I've ever had the pleasure of meeting you, Mrs. Rosso." He paused. "Conferences? Nope. Never received anything in the mail about parent-teacher conferences. No. Never."

"Yes, you did," I hissed. "I brought the letter home. You

just didn't see it. You lost it in all this . . . *crap!*" Tears of outrage were forming in the corners of my eyes.

"No," Dad said in a fake sad voice, "I'm afraid my busy schedule doesn't allow me the luxury of driving to Diamond in the middle of the day to meet a woman who gets her jollies playing power games with kids."

I ran to my bedroom and slammed the door. But even there I could hear Dad's obnoxious voice.

"And what *I'm* saying is that Benny is exempt from this requirement. I don't want him participating. Benny? Benny?"

"What?" I yelled from my room.

"Do not take anything out of this house!" Dad yelled back. "Nothing leaves this house. Do you understand me?"

I didn't answer. I couldn't. I just closed my eyes and listened to Dad's rabid craziness.

"Oh, really? He won't pass sixth grade if he doesn't do a service project? Don't be ridiculous. Oh, so *anything* around the house would be acceptable to you? Fine. He can help me build a motorcycle. Good-bye, Mrs. Rosso. Tell your husband he has my sympathy. What? You're divorced? I'm not surprised."

I was wrong. I could be madder at someone. And I was right then.

CHAPTER 9

MARCH MADNESS

MARCH WAS A LONG MONTH. It began cold and rainy and then turned warm and muddy.

School dragged on. After Dad's disastrous phone call to Mrs. Rosso, I found it hard to make eye contact with her during class. But Mrs. Rosso didn't hold it against me.

"You okay, Benny?" she asked almost every day. "Everything okay at home?"

I always nodded. How could I explain my home? How could I ask if it was possible to feel homesick in your own home?

One day after school, Mrs. Rosso handed me a blue Adidas bag full of clothes.

"Here," she said softly. "My nephew grows out of stuff like you wouldn't believe."

But I knew the clothes weren't from her nephew. They were brand new. One shirt still had the tags on it.

Mrs. Rosso gave me smaller things, too: notebooks, pens, M&M's, shampoo, a Speed Stick deodorant. If a person could die of embarrassment, I would've died if anyone knew my teacher was giving me personal hygiene products. Fortunately, Mrs. Rosso was sneaky. Nobody was curious about the manila envelopes she left on my desk with the words "French Revolution Extra Credit" written on the front.

Myron gave me ten dollars a week for my work at the radio station. I mailed four ten-dollar bills to the phone company in early March, hoping Mom would call again. She did. Mom called twice that month, both times from pay phones. It was hard to hear her, but she said the plan was still the same. She was going to come get me when school let out for summer, and then I'd go back to Louisiana with her.

"You'll be able to play with your cousins here," she said. "You remember your cousins, Gerald and Stevie? You liked them, remember?"

I'd met Mom's sister's kids only once when they came to visit. I was five. They'd poured Tabasco on my chocolate pudding.

Mom always talked about the beignets in New Orleans, and how much I'd love them. She also asked how piano lessons were going. I lied and said they were fine.

Every conversation with Mom ended with the same

question: "Has Dad thrown anything away?" But she already knew the answer: *No.*

The truer answer might've been: "Jesus H. Christ, Mom! If you thought the house was bad when you left, you should see it now."

Our house had gone from looking bad to looking awful. In addition to visiting the scrap yard to find parts to build a motorcycle, Dad had been hitting the county dump. Every few days he brought home another truckload of stuff. Broken chairs, moldy books, stained mattresses. Any unredeemable thing under the sun. It all came to our house.

When a dairy farmer in Neosho saw Dad scrounging around at the dump, he asked if Dad wanted to clean out his barn for fifty dollars. Dad jumped at the chance. He spent a week there and brought home several truckloads of broken tools, rusty varmint traps, empty paint cans, and a ladder missing half its rungs. Other farmers in the area found out about Dad and started hiring him to clean out their barns, too.

One day I came home from school to find that Dad had taken all the doors in our house off their hinges and stacked them in my bedroom.

"Only a temporary arrangement," he said.

"Dad, I need a door on my room," I said. "I need to be able to close my door."

"Mr. Privacy, eh?" he said sarcastically. "When you pay the bills around here, you can arrange the house any way you like. Until then, I need the extra space. A swinging door takes up a lot of room. Relax, will you? It's just until I find a new place to rent for Calvin's Collectibles."

But he wasn't even looking for a place to rent. And I *was* paying the bills, or at least one of them. But I couldn't tell Dad about the phone bill without telling him about Mom's calls, and I didn't want to get into all that.

Another day I came home to find a pile of old, moth-eaten school band uniforms stuffed in my bathtub. I pulled them out and carried them to the hall where I dumped them in a dusty heap. Three mice popped out of the pile and made a mad dash for the kitchen.

Join the club, I thought.

We had lots of mice by then. Roaches, too. The unlucky ones were floating in the clogged kitchen sink.

Around this time, Dad discovered a discount grocery store on Highway 71. He started bringing home bags of puffed wheat cereal, bruised bananas, generic cola, and gallons of spoiled milk. When I pointed out the expiration date on the milk, Dad scoffed.

"Don't you know that's just a trick grocery stores play on gullible people to make them throw out perfectly good food?" He tore open a carton and drank from it. "See? It's fine. Delicious. You should drink more milk, Benny. Calcium. Good for your bones."

The dishwasher was still broken. The moldy pizza boxes

were still stacked in the kitchen corner. The refrigerator was filled with rotten food and foul milk. But we still ate dinner together every night. Dad said that was important.

"We're a team, Benny," he often said. "It's us against them."

We ate bowl after bowl of popcorn, always in the living room. I sat on the sturdiest cardboard box. Dad had his spot on the sofa. The TV was always on somewhere, though I couldn't see it. Piles of junk were in the way. I could only hear the endless drone of feuding characters on *Dallas, Dynasty,* and *Falcon Crest.*

One night when we were eating, I heard a drip and looked up. The roof was leaking. A dark stain shaped like a birthmark was spreading across the ceiling.

Dad quickly moved from the couch and started rummaging through a pile. He found a plastic shower curtain and pulled it out. He shook it and then draped it lovingly over his Tandy computer.

"Gotta protect Mount Tandy," he said in all seriousness. "The great and powerful Mount Tandy."

Maybe it was good that Mom wasn't around to see all this.

CHAPTER 10

BREAKING EGGS, BREAKING NEWS

IT WAS WARM FOR EASTER, which fell that year on the first Sunday in April. Dad didn't want to go to the Easter service. After Mom left, he'd pretty much stopped going to church. On Easter Sunday he said he was too busy with the motorcycle.

"I've almost got this thing running," he said as I was leaving for church. "I can't stop now."

Fine with me, I thought. I was mainly going for the egg roll after church. It was always fun to see the pettiness, cheating, and downright ruthlessness that arose out of people who had just celebrated the risen Lord.

"All right," Preacher Huffman said after the service, "everyone listen to Verna for instructions."

We were gathered—forty-some people—in the grass between church and the church hall.

"Does everyone have a hard-boiled egg?" Mrs. Verna Hartzell asked. "If you don't, now's the time to get one. I dyed five dozen eggs, so I know there's enough for everyone, including Ringo, who I imagine has eaten half a dozen by now."

She would never forgive Myron's dog for dragging her cats around by their neck fat.

"Now," she continued, "men and boys, line up on the church side of the yard. Women and girls, stay on this side."

"The battle of the sexes," Myron observed gleefully. He and Ringo were wearing matching purple bandannas for Easter.

Mrs. Hartzell glared at him. "I will remind everyone," she said, curling her lip, "that even though we are outside, we are still in God's eyesight and earshot. So let's please keep our hearts and tongues clean, for His sake as well as ours."

"How's this egg roll work again?" Mayor Roland Prell asked. "I can never remember."

"It's simple," Mrs. Crumple said from the ladies' side of the yard. "We take turns rolling eggs toward the center of the yard. Your side rolls an egg and our side rolls an egg. You want the eggs to hit. Whoever's egg cracks is out."

"That's right," said Preacher Huffman. "Because only one egg will crack. It's the miracle of Jesus."

"C'mon, let's start!" whooped one-armed Dallas Emery.

He always took great pride in doing well in the egg rolls. Most everyone had forgiven him for the year he brought a white marble egg to the competition. He got to the final round before anyone realized why his egg wasn't cracking.

"All right, we're ready for our first rollers," Mrs. Hartzell announced. "Ladies, pick someone. Gentlemen, you choose, too."

It was Myron versus Mrs. Crumple. I took a step behind Mayor Prell. I'd been hiding from Mrs. Crumple for months, ever since I missed my first piano lesson.

"One," Mrs. Hartzell said, holding up her index finger. "Two. Three. Roll!"

Mrs. Crumple swooped low and rolled her egg with dignity. She looked like a retired ballerina. Myron rolled his egg like he was at a bowling alley. Ringo ran after both eggs and swallowed them whole, shell and all.

"Disqualified!" Mrs. Hartzell proclaimed, either outraged or delighted. I couldn't tell which.

"Aw heck, Ringo," Myron complained. "Sorry about that, Mrs. Crumple!"

"Not a problem," Mrs. Crumple answered with a smile. She'd had a respectable roll, and that's all that really mattered.

"Get over here, Ringo," Myron demanded.

The guilty but thrilled dog ran across the yard, dragging his belly in the grass and thumping his tail. Everyone laughed except Mrs. Hartzell. Ringo jumped up and licked her face in passing.

"Get that dog *out* of here!" Mrs. Hartzell commanded.

Next up were Izzy and Carmen.

"I want to beat you," Carmen said with a wicked smile, "because you've been delivering mail to my restaurant later and later."

"You talk a good game," Izzy sneered, "but let's see what you've got."

"One," Mrs. Hartzell said, holding up a finger. "Two. Three. Roll!"

Carmen hurled her egg with vengeance toward the center of the yard. Izzy took two giant steps forward and did the same.

"Cheater!" Carmen yelled. "He cheated! Did you see what he did? He waited till I rolled, then *he* rolled. It's a trick!"

"I didn't do anything wrong, did I, Mrs. Hartzell?" Izzy asked.

"You weren't standing far enough back," Mrs. Hartzell replied sternly. "But that was my mistake. I forgot to mark the starting lines." She looked around and saw me. "Benny, run down to the basement of the church hall and get me two pieces of rope."

I did as told. The church hall basement was musty and damp, but everything was neatly stacked and labeled on shelves. *Christmas ornaments* were next to *Santa Suit. Badminton Rackets + Net* were next to *Tablecloths (Square)* and *Tablecloths (Round).*

I couldn't find any rope so I grabbed two rulers from the *Yardsticks/Rulers* shelf. I ran with them up the stairs and out in the yard.

"Will these work?" I asked, handing the rulers to Mrs. Hartzell. I noticed while standing under her that she had several whiskers on her chin like a man—or a cat.

"Yes," she said. "Put one on either side. Now listen closely, everyone. You must stand behind the rulers. Izzy and Carmen, roll again."

Izzy and Carmen stood across from each other with their replacement eggs. They rolled. Carmen ran to the center of the yard to see the results.

"Izzy's egg is cracked! Izzy's egg is cracked!" Carmen chanted, holding up her opponent's egg and wiggling her bottom.

"Izzy is eliminated from the competition," Mrs. Hartzell announced. "Carmen has made it to the next round."

Carmen danced her way to the back of the ladies' line. Izzy retreated to the sideline, muttering something about overpriced enchiladas.

I looked around for Myron and Ringo. They weren't there. And since I'd forgotten my egg in the church hall basement, I wandered away from the competition and around the corner to Myron's shop.

Lately on Sundays he'd been playing *Jesus Christ Superstar* and *Quadrophenia*. Between the two albums, there were four records. It gave Myron time to run errands, hit a nearby flea market, or go to church if he felt like it. And if the music ended before he got back to the station? He just apologized for the interruption, flipped the stack of records over, and played the B sides. It's not like his listening audience was going to complain, especially on a Sunday when almost everyone was at church.

So when I opened Myron's shop door I was surprised to hear his voice coming through several radios in the front room. Who could he possibly be interviewing on Easter Sunday? Only as I walked toward the back of the shop did I realize he wasn't doing an interview. He was announcing something.

I poked my head around the kitchen door and saw Myron sitting in a chair. His eyes were closed. His face was serious. He was leaning back so far that the chair was balanced on two legs. He was holding the microphone right up to his mouth.

"It's the bottom of the ninth, and the score is two runs apiece for the Cardinals and the Cubs. St. Louis needs this win. Let's see if slugger Myron Kazie can work his magic. Last year the KZ Kid, as he's called, hit .356 and drove in a hundred and fifteen runs. Mighty impressive for the slugger from tiny Dennis Acres, that little town of big dreams. The pitcher, Calvin Summer, winds up, throws, and it's STEE-RIKE ONE. Kazie is not happy with that call. But he's shaking it off. Yes, he is. And now here's the windup and the pitch. Kazie swings and . . . he hits it! It's going deep into the outfield.

This ball's going back! Back, back, back! This one's going all the way. I don't know if we'll ever see this ball again, folks! *Adios!* Leave it to Myron Kazie to hit the game-winning round-tripper in the bottom of the—"

I couldn't help it. I was laughing. Myron opened his eyes and saw me.

"Oh," he said, putting his chair back on solid ground. "I didn't know anyone was listening."

"You're good," I said. "You're really good."

"Thanks," Myron replied, grinning widely. "You want in the game?"

"Yeah!"

Myron closed his eyes again and turned on his baseball announcer voice.

"Critics are calling it a trick, a hoax, an optical illusion. But Benny Summer has the magic touch, folks, there's no doubt about it. So far this year he's pitched seventeen no-hitters, and it doesn't look like anything or anyone will stop him. The kid's got such a supple wrist. Magic fingers, man."

I laughed. Myron opened his eyes.

"Keep going," I said.

Myron continued. "He's a good-lookin' kid, tall, about six feet one, lean and mean at a hundred and eighty."

I was holding my stomach, I was laughing so hard. I was one of the tallest kids in my class, but nowhere near six feet tall or a hundred and eighty pounds. Last time we had to get on a scale in health class, I weighed seventy-two pounds.

"But boy, can this kid pitch," Myron said, his eyes still closed. "Curveballs, fastballs, rising fastballs with a twist of lemon-lime. He can do 'em all, and when he does, the crowd goes wild. Just listen to 'em roar as Benny walks out on the field! He waves, tips his hat. Always a gentleman, this Summer kid."

I heard the cowbells clang above the shop door. Myron must've heard them, too, because he straightened up.

"We (*ahem*) hope you've enjoyed this special broadcast," Myron said into the microphone. "And now we'll return to side three of *Quadrophenia* by the British group known simply as The Who."

He dropped the needle on the record. We tiptoed out of the kitchen and closed the door.

I was still laughing when I saw Miss Tina Turnipson standing in Myron's front room. Her face was deathly white. Her eyes were red. Clearly she was going to either cry or vomit.

"You won't believe it," Miss Turnipson said. "You just won't believe it."

"What?" Myron asked. "Are you okay? What is it?"

"I don't know what we're going to do," she said, shaking her head. "This is a disaster. It's all my fault." She burst into tears.

"Just take your time, Tina, and tell me what it is," Myron pleaded.

"I was at my grandparents' house for Easter," she said through her tears. "They live in Tulsa. I just got home a little while ago and found this in my mailbox." She held out a piece of paper like it was a dead squirrel. "Read it for yourself."

Myron's eyes quickly scanned the page. "What? *How?*"

"I don't *know!*" Miss Turnipson wailed. "It must've been my essay or that stupid drawing. But we won! Dennis Acres won the America's Most Charming Small Town contest."

"Why's that bad?" I asked.

"Because," sobbed Miss Turnipson, "it means representatives from the U.S. Chamber of Commerce are coming here in five weeks to meet us in person. They'll find out we're not what I said we were. They'll find out what a *miserable* little town Dennis Acres really is."

"Aw, shoot," Myron said. "It's not that bad here, is it?"

"Yes, it *is!*" Miss Turnipson cried. "It's ugly as sin and dull as dishwater! And now everyone's going to know. We'll be the laughingstock of America!"

CHAPTER 11

LOOK WHO'S TALKING (WITH TINA TURNIPSON)

BY TUESDAY, WORD HAD GOTTEN around town.

"It's *so* exciting," Stormy whispered to me before Social Studies. "Makes me wish I lived in Dennis Acres 'stead of on Highway V."

"You should move," I whispered back. "Get somebody to pull your trailer down the highway and park it in Dennis Acres."

She laughed. "I'll ask my mom."

"Has she found a job yet?"

Stormy shook her head. "Still looking."

Her service project was going no better than mine.

"I'll help you think of more job ideas," I said. "After school?"

It was my cowardly way of inviting her to sit next to me on the bus after school. But as usual, Stormy sat in the front of the bus and I sat in the back by myself. That is, until Miss Tina Turnipson slid in beside me.

"Do you think Myron has the phones working yet?" she asked nervously.

I was trying to catch Stormy's eye, but she didn't see me. Chance and Rance were sitting in the seat behind her, tapping her on the shoulder and then laughing and looking innocent when she turned around. It was the oldest trick in the book, but I couldn't tell if Stormy thought it was dumb or funny. Man, I hated those Ants brothers.

"Well, does he?" Miss Turnipson pressed.

"Huh?" I replied. "I mean, yeah. My dad helped him run the phone lines. If people want to call in during your show, Myron can put them on the air. He's got three phones that'll take calls simultaneously."

"Oh," Miss Turnipson said darkly.

Now Lance was getting in on the fun. He was trying to impress Stormy by showing her his golden tooth. *Big whoop.* If I'd broken a molar chewing rocks, I don't think I'd be so quick about showing it off. I was glad Mrs. Rosso had rejected his idea of updating the sidewalk crack count for his service project.

When Stormy got off the bus, the Ants brothers moved to

the back so they could make smoochy noises at me and Miss Turnipson. I ignored them.

Twenty-five minutes later we arrived at the radio station. Myron was scribbling questions on a pad of paper.

"Hey," he said, looking up. "I don't usually prepare for interviews, but I figure we've got a lot of ground to cover today. So, have a seat, Tina. Make yourself comfortable. Benny, get some water for Miss Turnipson, will you? And get ready to transcribe this show."

At four o'clock on the dot, Myron played the "Turn It Up with Tina Turnipson" theme song. I always wondered if Miss Turnipson realized it was a jazzy rendition of "Here Comes Peter Cottontail Hoppin' Down the Bunny Trail." There was something undeniably rabbity about her.

"Good afternoon, Dennis Acres," Myron said as he faded out the music. "Welcome to another edition of 'Turn It Up with Tina Turnipson.' And have we got some news for you today. Why don't you tell us about it, Tina?"

Miss Turnipson cleared her throat importantly. "Well, it's hard to believe, but our little town of Dennis Acres has been named America's Most Charming Small Town by the United States Chamber of Commerce. Representatives from that fine organization will arrive on Monday, May ninth, from Washington, D.C., to present us with a framed certificate."

"Nothing wrong with that," Myron said, helping her out.

Miss Turnipson wasn't listening. She was reading from a script she'd prepared.

"While our guests are here," she continued, "they'll conduct a site survey of the whole town. They'll want to see everyone's house—inside and out—because they're going to give every household a free computer." She took a nervous breath. "And then they're going to tie all the computers together with wires so we can talk to each other through the computers."

"Sounds interesting," said Myron tentatively.

"So," Miss Turnipson said, "I think it only makes sense for us to take some time today to discuss how we might spiff things up a bit before these important people from Washington arrive."

"Agreed," said Myron. "I bet you have some ideas on that score, Tina. And I wouldn't be surprised if our listeners do, too. Folks, if you want to join the conversation, just dial 555-6804. The phones lines are open. Tina, how do you propose we prepare for this event?"

"Well," she replied, smiling and setting her script aside, "I know it's just a little thing, but I bought a new shirt for Mr. Dallas Emery. I've noticed he likes to cut off one sleeve on all his shirts. I think it'd be nice if Mr. Emery had a shirt with *two* long sleeves. I'll stitch up the cuff on his, um, y'know, his *bad* arm, so it won't get in the way."

Myron was looking at Miss Turnipson like she'd just sprouted a second head.

"That's one idea," he said. "Let's hear from a caller, shall we. Hello? Oops. I think I cut someone off. Hope it wasn't poor Dallas Emery's other arm. Folks, if I cut you off, just call back, okay? I'm still getting the feel for this new system. Let's try this phone. Hello?"

"Dallas Emery here," the caller said.

"Dallas!" Myron said, laughing. "Good to hear from you, pal. What do you think of this award?"

"I don't give diddly-squat about awards," Mr. Dallas Emery barked. "I'm calling to say I don't have a *bad* arm. I have a *missing* arm. The only bad things I know of are the manners of the young lady you're interviewing. I say 'lady,' but no lady wears skirts as short as that gal."

Miss Turnipson nearly jumped out of her seat.

"What?" she shrieked. She looked like she'd stepped on a bee in her bare feet.

"And another thing," Mr. Dallas Emery said. "I've already got me a calculator. I've had it for two years."

"Now, Dallas," Myron said gently, "we're talking about computers here, not calculators. And I think Tina was just trying to . . . Dallas, are you there? I think he hung up. Let's try this line. Hello?"

"Hello, this is Verna Hartzell. I think our town is quite charming, and I'm glad someone else has finally noticed. One thing I suggest we tidy up before the hotshots from Washington arrive is Arthur Rayborn's garden. Can someone roll those tractor tires behind his house? They look tacky. Just my opinion."

"Noted, Verna," said Myron. He looked at me and raised his eyebrows to make sure I was making a note of Mrs. Hartzell's suggestion. Then he picked up another phone. "Let's see who we have here. Hello?"

"It's Art Rayborn. Tell Verna I'll get rid of my tires when she gets rid of her cats. It's a disgrace to have a house full of cats. Bet she has a dozen or fourteen cats in that house. I wouldn't be surprised if the judges revoke our award once they see Verna's cat house."

"'Preciate the call, Art," Myron said. His eyes and fingers were jumping between the three phones. Each phone had a flashing red light indicating a caller. He picked up another phone. "Hello?"

"It's Verna again. Tell Art I have *nine* cats. Nine! And every one of them is spayed or neutered and up to date on rabies and distemper shots, which is more than I can say for some people in this town."

"Okay, Verna," Myron said. "Thanks for the clarific—"

"And another thing," Mrs. Hartzell interrupted. "I wouldn't have to *have* a house for my cats if a certain dog didn't terrorize my cats night and day. I'm not naming names, but I think you know who I mean, Myron. Good-bye. Oh, and I don't need a new calculator, either. I prefer an adding machine. Or plain old paper and pencil. Bye now."

"Bye, Verna," said Myron. He was beginning to look frazzled. He picked up another phone. "Who's on this line?"

"I'd rather not say my name," the caller said. "But there's a resident of Dennis Acres who was born in Mexico, and I'm just wondering if everything's squared away with her immigration paperwork. You know, before the officials from Washington get here?"

"Gotcha, Izzy," Myron said. "Let me guess who this next caller will be. Carmen, are you there?"

"Yes, I'm here," Carmen replied hotly. "Tell Izzy that I am a legal resident of this country, and I have the papers to prove it. What I'd like to know is if he pays taxes on the money he makes heating up and delivering those god-awful frozen pizzas. If not, I think the people from Washington, D.C., would be very interested to hear that." She slammed down the phone.

Jeez-o-pete! I'd never heard people get so mad about winning a contest. If I'd had time, I would've passed a note to Myron, suggesting he ask everyone to take a deep breath and do twenty jumping jacks, like Mrs. Rosso had us do. But the phone calls didn't let up. I was shocked no one had mentioned Dad yet.

After fifteen more minutes of angry callers and finger pointers, Miss Tina Turnipson finally raised her voice.

"People!" she said sternly into her microphone. "That's *enough.* You sound like a bunch of sassy kindergartners. Now listen up and listen good. I'm sorry I got us into this mess. I really am. But representatives from the U.S. Chamber of Commerce will be here in thirty-four days. Every household is getting a free personal computer whether you want one or not. If you don't want them, fine. I'll come around and pick them up after our guests from Washington leave."

"I can help," added Myron, massaging his temples.

"But please, can we stay on topic here?" Miss Turnipson implored. "I didn't realize buying Mr. Dallas Emery a new shirt would be taken as an insult. But I can see now that we should all focus less on what's wrong with each other, and instead look at our own houses and selves and, yes, skirts to see what we can do to clean up our acts."

"Amen," Myron mumbled with his eyes closed. "And for the record, I think your skirts are fine."

Miss Turnipson barreled ahead. "That said, I think we can all agree there's one person in this town who might need help cleaning up his house and yard."

I stopped writing. Myron opened his eyes. Miss Turnipson was staring directly at him and smiling sweetly.

"I know, I know," Myron said with a heavy sigh. "And he is my best friend. Folks, I'll do what I can, okay? Benny can help." He looked at me. "You wouldn't mind helping me clean up your house, would you? Maybe this weekend?"

"No," I said, startled by the question. "I mean, yes. I'll help."

Getting rid of all the trash in our house would take days, maybe even weeks, but I was willing to tackle the job. After all, it was my original service project idea. As embarrassing as it was to have this broadcast all over town, it *was* a good idea. The only problem was, Dad would hate it.

CHAPTER 12

SERIOUSLY, MAN, CLEAN UP YOUR ACT

"AREN'T YOU SUPPOSED to be helping me?" Dad asked.

It was Saturday morning. Dad was making popcorn for breakfast.

"You need help making popcorn?" I asked.

"No. The motorcycle. I've almost got it running. I could use some help, though. And you need to do a service project, right?"

He had me there. Suddenly I was signed up for two service projects.

I didn't tell Dad about the plan to clean our house. I figured Myron could do that. I just followed Dad outside. My job was to hold the motorcycle upright while Dad laid on his back and worked on the engine.

"Motorcycle mechanics," Dad said, tightening something with a wrench. "Simple engineering when you think about it. But it all comes down to the rider."

"Uh-huh," I said.

I looked around our yard. Everyone else in Dennis Acres had already cut their grass once or twice. We didn't have much grass. Our yard was mainly weeds with piles here and there of dead car batteries, metal furniture, broken mowers, and rusty bikes. There were always three or four fat squirrels hanging around.

"It's all about balance, Benny," Dad was saying.

"Okay," I said, looking around for rats. I hated rats. Everything about them gave me the creeps, especially their scaly tails. Rats had taken over our root cellar, hoping to beat out the squirrels in the race for the stale popcorn Dad sometimes threw out the front door.

One night a rat got in the house. It must've crawled through an open window. I heard Dad yelling at it to get out. From the way he was shouting, I thought it was a burglar. I stayed in my room until it was quiet. When I found Dad in the living room, he said everything was fine. "Just a hungry rat," he'd said, closing the glass door on the Cornucopia popcorn maker. He sent me back to bed for endless hours of rat nightmares while he stayed in the dark and jungly living room. Nights like those were when I missed Mom the most.

My arms were getting tired. "Are you almost done?"

"When you're older, you're going to want to ride this thing," Dad said from under the motorcycle. "So pay attention. Learn how it works. The right hand is for acceleration. See that grip on the right? You twist it toward you to accelerate. If you want to brake, step on the right pedal. That's the rear wheel brake. The lever on the right handlebar operates the front brake. You've got to be careful with that one or you'll pitch yourself over the front of the bike."

I turned my head and looked at our house. It still reminded me of a rotten egg, but now it looked like a rotten egg that had been left outside to decompose. The color had changed from yellow to green to gray. Dad had covered the windows with cardboard on the inside to prevent anyone from seeing what was in the house. The more crap he accumulated, the more paranoid he became of someone stealing it. It didn't make sense. None of it made sense.

The phone was ringing inside. It might've been Mom. I wanted to go answer it, but Dad was still talking.

"The clutch is the lever just ahead of the left-hand grip. You need to pull that in when you shift gears with your left foot. Lift your foot up for first gear. Push down for all the other gears. It takes practice, but you'll get the hang of it."

I looked up and saw Myron walking toward the house. He was wearing old clothes and carrying a pair of heavy work gloves. Ringo trotted alongside him.

"Hey, Benny," he called.

"Hey, Myron," I called back. Already I was nervous about this scene.

Dad raised his head from under the motorcycle. He lifted his chin in greeting and then resumed his position under the bike.

"Nice ride," Myron said.

"Thanks," Dad grunted.

Myron dived right in. "So Calvin, have you heard the news? About this contest we won? It's crazy, I know, but folks from Washington will be here in a month. And we, uh . . . everybody, um . . . Well, I was just thinking it'd be a good excuse to pick up a bit around here, inside and out. Nice day for it, too."

Dad didn't answer, so Myron kept going.

"I mean, would you mind kinda, y'know, tidying up a little around, y'know, here?" Myron laughed at his own sputtering. "I'd be willing to help. I bet Benny would, too. Right, Benny?"

"Uh-huh," I said, staring at the motorcycle. This wasn't going well.

Dad didn't respond, so Myron kept talking.

"Seriously, man," he said. "You've got to clean up your act, and this would be as good a time as any to do it. People in town are, uh, well, y'know, talking about your place."

Dad craned his neck sideways so he could see Myron. "What do I care what anybody in Dennis Acres thinks about me? Everybody knows who I am and what my place looks like."

"But the people coming aren't *from* Dennis Acres," Myron put in quickly. "They're from the U.S. Chamber of Commerce in Washington, D.C."

Dad was now squinting into the sun. "What do I care what people who don't even know me think about me?"

Myron and I looked at each other and shrugged. You couldn't argue with my dad. He'd get you coming and going.

"Well," Myron said, saluting, "I said I'd try and I tried. Come on, Ringo. Oh, wait. Calvin, did you hear every household in town is going to get a free computer? Pretty cool, eh?"

Dad made a sour face. "I already have one."

"I know," Myron said. "But now you'll have another."

"I hope you don't think I'm going to teach everybody in Dennis Acres how to operate a computer," Dad snarled. "Because I'm not. I'll teach you and Benny. That's it."

Myron smiled and nodded. "Okay. See you guys later."

An hour later Miss Turnipson arrived. She was wearing one of her shorter skirts. Dad was sitting in the grass now, still working on the motorcycle.

"Well, if it isn't the Summer boys," Miss Turnipson said, smiling like a cheerleader.

Dad didn't say hello or even look at her.

"Mr. Summer," she began, "I don't know if you've heard, but—"

"I'm not putting on lipstick for your Chamber of Commerce friends," Dad said coldly without taking his eyes off the motorcycle.

She laughed. "We're not asking you to wear lipstick. Just to clean up a little. And I'd be happy to put together a committee to help. If we spent just one day here, I bet we could—"

"Get arrested for trespassing," Dad said flatly. "Don't think I wouldn't do it."

Mayor Roland Prell arrived by car later that afternoon. Dad was still tinkering with the motorcycle.

"We'll condemn it, Calvin," Mayor Prell said. He was a square-shaped man with a round pink face. "We'll tear down the house. Or we could burn it to the ground. That'd be cheaper and it'd take care of the rats."

"You'd have to burn it with me in there," Dad said casually, nodding with his head toward our house. "And that would be murder. I'd like to see you campaign some year from jail. Now that'd be interesting. Better than your usual Mayberry RFD–style campaign. A little folksy for my taste, Mayor."

Mayor Prell blew out a big puff of air. "Calvin Summer, why do you insist on being so difficult? Hmm? I'd like to know. Tell me. Why?"

Dad just smiled.

"I'm not leaving until you give me an answer," Mayor Prell said. His pink face was turning red.

Dad finally stood up. He stretched his arms lazily above

his head and scratched his greasy hair with his long finger-nails. Then he walked over to an old parking meter he'd found at the dump. It was leaning against our only tree. He looked at the parking meter as if he were studying it.

"I'm afraid to tell you, Mayor Prell, but your time here has expired. If you'd like to stay in my yard and chat longer, you'll have to deposit a quarter. Otherwise I'm going to call Deputy Rodney and have you removed from my castle."

"Your *castle*?" Mayor Prell asked. He practically spat out the word.

"A man's home is his castle," Dad replied, stroking his beard. "And you're not welcome at my castle."

Mayor Prell's car tires squealed down the street. Dad smiled a scary smile and walked over to the motorcycle. He threw a leg over the seat and kick-started the engine with his foot. With his right hand he revved the engine loud.

"They wouldn't dare, Benny," Dad yelled over the roar. "They wouldn't dare."

CHAPTER 13

THE GREAT PIANO RECITAL PLOT

IT WAS MRS. CRUMPLE'S IDEA. She told us the next day after church.

"Benny needs to be in this year's piano recital," she informed Myron during the coffee hour.

I nearly choked on a stale snickerdoodle. Myron saw my distress.

"A piano recital?" he said. "I don't know, Mrs. Crumple. That seems—"

"Listen to me," she said firmly. "I'll teach him an easy song and put him at the end of the program. We always begin the recital with a reception. Punch, cookies, nothing fancy. By the time I have all my students play a song and pose for photographs, it's a good two hours. I could stretch it to two and a half hours if I had to." She paused for dramatic effect. "Do you think we could get Calvin to attend?"

"A piano recital?" Myron repeated. "I don't know, Mrs. Crumple."

She leaned in close to Myron. "Because if we could get Calvin here for a few hours . . ." Her pause invited Myron to finish the thought.

"Some of us could clean his house," Myron said slowly.

"And yard," Mrs. Crumple added. "You'll need two or three pickup trucks. I'll call the dump and tell them to expect several large loads." She took a sip of coffee while her eyes scanned the room as if dividing the congregation into spies and allies.

"Mrs. Crumple, you're a genius," Myron said. "A diabolical genius."

"It's my cross to bear," she replied curtly. "The recital is always on the first Saturday in May. That's just two days before our guests arrive from Washington, D.C."

"Cutting it close," Myron said. "But I don't see an alternative."

"Nor do I," said Mrs. Crumple. Her eyebrows arched like two lightning bolts.

They were both forgetting one thing.

"Dad would be furious," I said.

Mrs. Crumple clucked her tongue. "This is no longer

about your father, Benny, or his misplaced pride. It's about the pride of Dennis Acres."

"But if you throw away his stuff," I said, "he'll go nuts. He'll go crazy."

Myron put his arm around my shoulder. "We'll just get rid of the unredeemables. The stuff that's truly worthless. He'll be mad at first, I know. But when he sees how much better the place looks? Really, I think he'll be grateful."

"And if he's not," Mrs. Crumple said with a snort, "tough toenails."

"But . . . but . . . but," I stammered. "There's another reason this won't work."

"What?" Myron and Mrs. Crumple asked at the same time.

"I don't know how to play the piano. Dad thinks I've been taking lessons since January. He'll expect me to be good."

"I can teach you," Mrs. Crumple promised with a flutter of her hand. "That will be the easy part." She hummed a happy little tune as she turned briskly on her heel and rejoined the covey of ladies gathered around the Mr. Coffee machine.

I staggered back to the radio station with Myron. "I don't think I can learn to play a song in a month. And it's not even a whole month, Myron. It's less than a month. I don't think I can do it. In fact, I know I *can't* do it."

Myron was listening and nodding. When we got to the station, he turned the *Quadrophenia* record over and moved the needle to the last song, the one he liked best. It was called "Love Reign O'er Me."

"Shh," he whispered, turning up the volume. "Listen."

He sat down in a kitchen chair and closed his eyes. I slumped in the chair across from him. The song began with piano music and the sound of rain falling, but then the singer started screaming. I wasn't sure if it was supposed to be a pretty song or an angry one. Screaming about love for five minutes— this racket counted as music? Myron had the stereo turned up so loud, it hurt my head just to listen.

But when the song ended, I saw that Myron was crying. Not big blubbery Miss Turnipson–style sobs, but two thin tears were rolling down his cheeks. He took off his glasses and wiped the tears away with the back of his hand. Then he moved the stereo needle to the first song and motioned for me to join him in the front room.

"Music is a powerful thing, Benny," he said. "It's the highest art form. I think it's the only thing I really believe in." He rubbed his eyes. "Learn how to play the piano. You'll never regret it."

"I *can't* learn how to play the piano in a month!"

"Then try the guitar," Myron said. "Pete Townshend, the guy who wrote *Quadrophenia*, started playing guitar when he was twelve. How old are you?"

"Twelve. But I can't learn how to play the piano *or* the guitar in the next month."

"You don't have to," he said, ignoring the looming dead-line. "But just promise me you'll learn someday."

"Okay, but not before Mrs. Crumple's recital. Please!" I was getting frantic.

"Fair enough," he said. "In that case we have to come up with another plan."

And we did.

CHAPTER 14

FRAUD ELISE

IT WAS HOT THAT SATURDAY, unusually hot for May, and the church hall didn't have air-conditioning. Mrs. Crumple asked Preacher Huffman to drive over to the funeral home in Diamond to pick up a box of shell-shaped cardboard fans with the grim reminder "It's Only His (Her) Shell" printed on the front.

Earlier in the week when I told Dad that I'd be playing Beethoven's "Für Elise" in the recital, he looked up from his computer and said, "On the piano?"

"Yeah," I said. "You should come."

"How long's it going to last?"

"An hour or so," I said. "It starts at four o'clock with a reception."

I knew Dad didn't like to leave the house. He worried constantly about burglars. Whenever he went to the dump or junkyard, he wore at least two wristwatches so he could keep track of the time. He was convinced anyone who broke into our house would need at least an hour to find the best treasures. So he'd leave his collection unprotected for an hour, but rarely longer than that.

"You don't practice much," Dad observed.

We both looked at the piano in the corner of the living room. It was only partly visible under a heap of clothes, magazines, and a broken exercise bike. The piano bench was on the opposite side of the room. The TV was still parked on top of it.

"'Für Elise' isn't that hard to play," I lied.

"Huh," Dad muttered. "Will Nola be there?"

I wasn't expecting this. I didn't know how to answer. Did Dad want to see Mom? He couldn't. Otherwise he would've thrown away his holy splinter months ago, when she asked him to. So why was he suddenly asking about Mom?

"Mom?" I asked, stalling. I hadn't heard from her in weeks.

"Yeah. Is Nola coming?"

What should I say? I searched my mind for an answer both vague and definitive enough to satisfy Dad.

"When pigs fly," I said, taking a chance.

Dad's mouth curled into the old familiar smirk.

He insisted on riding his motorcycle to the recital, probably just to bug everyone. It would've been quicker to walk, but Dad wanted to show me how easily the motorcycle started now.

"See?" he said, pulling in the clutch and kick-starting the engine. "Kid stuff. Get on the back."

The cleanup crew was waiting behind Carmen's Casita. I never found out who all was there. I was told later that everyone who wasn't at the recital was instructed to meet at Carmen's at four o'clock sharp. Myron had my key to the house.

Inside the church hall, my nerves turned to nausea when I saw the crowd. I was surprised how many people were there and how many I didn't recognize. They must've been from nearby towns. I looked around for Stormy, hoping I wouldn't see her. I didn't.

Dad sat on a folding chair in the last row. He was fanning himself with a recital program and scowling.

"You want some punch or cookies or anything?" I asked.

"Nah," he said. "We'll have popcorn when this is over."

His hair was long and greasy. His beard looked ratty. He was wearing his worn-out *Star Trek* T-shirt. I knew he wouldn't get cleaned up for the recital. I bet he hadn't taken a shower in a month.

At four-thirty, Mrs. Crumple began asking everyone to

take their seats. All the performers, including me, sat in front in chairs turned sideways to the audience so that we were facing the back of the piano.

"Now I know some of our performers are nervous," Mrs. Crumple told the audience. "Some might even feel butterflies in their stomachs."

Butterflies? I had bats in my belly.

"So let's remember," Mrs. Crumple continued, "to show our appreciation by applauding after every song."

If I hadn't been so sick to my stomach with nervousness, I might've enjoyed seeing the Ants brothers in their clip-on ties. I had no idea they took piano lessons. They each played a classical song and then as a trio they performed a jazzy number called "Here Comes the Circus Train!" Chance sang "All aboooooard" while Lance hooted "woo woo" and Rance did some goofy leg movements that were supposed to mimic the wheels on a moving train. They didn't look nearly as mortified as I would've been. Truth is, they looked like they were enjoying themselves.

Mrs. Verna Hartzell played a long number from the *Nutcracker Suite*. I didn't know she took lessons. Even Preacher Huffman played "Simple Gifts."

My brain kept jumping from the scene in front of me to what I imagined was happening at our house. What would people think when they saw how we lived? Some of the piles in the living room now reached the ceiling. It'd gotten so bad you couldn't walk through the house unless you stayed on a narrow path that zigzagged through the forest of junk.

I hoped everyone knew not to throw away Dad's computer or any of his computer magazines. Or the Cornucopia popcorn maker. Or his vintage board games. Myron knew what to save and what to throw out. But did everybody else?

The plan was for Myron to get the cleanup crew started right at four o'clock. He'd fill as many truckloads as he could, but he promised to return to his shop at six o'clock. He and Mrs. Crumple had it all arranged. She was going to call him at his shop before four o'clock. He'd answer the phone in the front room. They'd leave the line open so Myron could hear when I was introduced. Mrs. Crumple said it wouldn't be before six-fifteen. Myron had Beethoven's *Greatest Hits* on the turntable ready to play. Mrs. Crumple had a transistor radio tuned to 88.1 FM sitting on the piano behind a large bust of Beethoven.

I looked at Dad in the back row. He had a gloomy, faraway look in his eye. I knew he was miserable sitting in that sweltering church hall. He would've been happier at home, protecting his stuff.

It was only then, as I sat waiting for my turn at the piano, that I realized what an awful mistake this was. What a terrible trick. I knew in that moment how devastated Dad would be when he discovered that Myron and the others had thrown away his collectibles. Sure, maybe to Myron they were unredeemables, but to Dad they were treasures. To Dad even a leaning tower of moldy pizza boxes was valuable.

It was all Myron's fault. If only he'd kept selling Dad the unredeemables for five dollars a box, our house wouldn't be such a disaster. Broken clock radios didn't stink or take up much room—not as much as junk from the dump did. And if Myron hadn't cooked up that ridiculous radio séance, Dad would never have started going to the junkyard looking for motorcycle parts.

No, it was Miss Turnipson's fault. If she hadn't entered Dennis Acres in that stupid contest, no one would've cared what our house looked like.

But really it was Mrs. Crumple's fault. She never should've suggested such a cruel-hearted trick. How would she like it if someone threw away her piano?

And then there was Mom. If only she hadn't left. If only she hadn't given Dad that ultimatum about the splinter. She knew how hard it was for him to get rid of things.

What if someone in the cleanup crew threw away Dad's holy splinter? There was no telling where Dad had it squirreled away. If someone threw it out, Dad would freak. He would flip. He would crack.

And whose fault would it be? Mine.

Because we were a team, Dad and me. It was us against them. He was counting on me, and I'd let him down. He would never forgive me for taking part in this treacherous plot.

I would've put an end to it right then if I could have. I would've yelled STOP at the top of my lungs if I thought it would do any good. But it was too late. Myron and his crew probably had two pickup trucks filled with Dad's stuff already. The plan was in motion. This grand scheme that had grown bigger than all of us was already stirring the atmosphere, re-arranging the molecules in some big and mysterious way. I could feel the terrifying intensity in the air. I could feel it tingling in my fingertips.

When Mrs. Crumple called my name, I took a deep, sick breath and walked to the piano. I sat on the bench and placed my fingers lightly on the keys. A tense silence followed as I watched Mrs. Crumple turn on the radio with her thumb-nail. She nudged the microphone gently in the direction of the tiny speaker.

As the simple melody began to play on the radio, I hunched my back in an attempt to hide my hands. I wasn't even close to replicating the correct fingering, but no one was laughing or giggling. Or pointing. Or even paying attention. I glanced out into the audience and saw a lot of closed eyes and cardboard fans flapping in front of hot faces.

For three long minutes I pretended to play "Für Elise." And then when the song was almost over, it happened. The music cut off. It was replaced by the sound of static, a high hum, and these words spoken by what sounded like a robot:

"This is the Emergency Broadcast System. The National Weather Service has issued a tornado warning for the following counties in Missouri: Barry, Lawrence, and Newton. At five-forty-five P.M., a tornado was spotted in southeast Oklahoma moving toward the Missouri border. This is not a test."

CHAPTER 15

THIS IS NOT A TEST

THE DOZING AUDIENCE SPRANG TO LIFE.

"A tornado? Where?"

"How fast is it moving? What direction?"

"Quiet!" Mrs. Crumple hollered, pulling the radio out in full view and holding it in front of the microphone. "Listen!"

"Large damaging hail up to baseball size is also possible," the robot voice said. "This storm is moving east at approximately forty miles per hour. An additional storm capable of producing a tornado is currently located in McDonald County and will move into Newton County over the next half hour."

"Oh my God!" someone screamed.

"What do we do?" someone else yelled.

"Be quiet!" Mrs. Crumple shouted.

She raised the radio up above her head, out of reach of the microphone. Everyone in the room had to be perfectly silent to hear.

"Move to an interior bathroom, closet, or hallway on the lowest floor of your building," the radio voice instructed. "Cover yourself with blankets, pillows, or a mattress for protection. If you are in a trailer or mobile home, seek other shelter immediately."

Folding chairs were falling to the floor as people pushed them out of their way. Parents were running for their frightened children. Someone was shrieking.

Preacher Huffman started shouting. "Go to the basement! Everybody go to the basement. Now!"

"We're going back to Diamond," a man said. I didn't recognize him.

"No time," Preacher Huffman said. "Everyone in the basement."

"But we don't go to church here!" someone else hollered.

"This is everyone's church now!" Preacher Huffman yelled. "In the basement, please. The stairs are over there. Hurry! Careful. No need to panic."

People began running toward the basement door and disappearing down the steps. I could hear heavy rain pelting the roof.

The church hall door opened with a whoosh. It was Myron.

He was with Carmen, Miss Turnipson, and Mayor Prell. Their clothes were drenched. Myron's eyes met Preacher Huffman's.

"You heard?" Myron asked. Panic was in his voice. "Everyone needs to take cover right away."

"Yes," Preacher Huffman answered. "We're moving everyone to the basement."

"Good," said Myron. "I told the cleanup crew to come down here."

"Plenty of room for everyone," Preacher Huffman said.

"Right," Myron replied, turning toward the door. "I'll be back in a minute. I have to get Ringo."

"No," Preacher Huffman said quietly, putting his hand on Myron's back.

"I can't leave Ringo alone," Myron said. "He hates storms."

The rain was getting louder. "I need your help here," Preacher Huffman said, looking around. He raised his voice again. "Move to the basement, please! Myron will help anyone down the steps who needs assistance."

I watched Dad make his way toward the door.

"Calvin!" Preacher Huffman boomed.

"I have a house," Dad said. "Two doors down."

"I'd rather you join us in the basement," Preacher Huffman said evenly. "Please."

"Thanks, but no thanks," Dad grumbled. He was standing in the doorway, looking quizzically at the trucks parked in front of our house. "Come on, Benny."

"But we don't have a basement," I said.

"We have a root cellar," Dad answered.

"A root cellar with *rats*," I cried.

Hail was falling. It was beating down on the church hall roof. It was bouncing in the street. It looked like someone was flying over Dennis Acres in a plane, dumping thousands of icy ping-pong balls. The sky was dark green and yellow, the same rotten-egg color as our house.

"Come on, Benny," Dad repeated. "We're going home. We'll get the bike tomorrow."

Feeling both stupid and loyal, I followed Dad out the door. We were instantly soaked. The rain was falling like a wall of water. I covered my head with my hands and sprinted.

When we got to the house, I ran up on the porch for cover. Dad was standing on the sidewalk, looking at the three pickup trucks left by the cleanup crew. Then he turned and roared up the porch steps. I followed him inside the house.

"What the hell?" Dad screamed, a look of horror in his eyes. "Someone's been in here. Someone's been stealing my collectibles!"

"Not stealing," I yelled. "Cleaning!"

Rain was pelting the roof. The windows and doors rattled. I could hear glass breaking somewhere.

Dad ran back outside and began tearing madly into the trash bags in the pickup trucks.

"Dad!" I yelled from the porch. He didn't answer, so I ran

out in the yard. "Dad!" It was hard to keep my eyes open against the driving force of the wind and the rain. "Daaaaad!"

I had to shout above the roar of the rain. But even then, he wasn't listening to me. He was screaming and swearing and pulling things from the trash bags. He was making a pile of junk in our muddy yard.

"Daaaaaaad!" I yelled again. The wind roared. The tree in our front yard was doing a backbend.

"I've got to save my collection!" Dad bellowed in a shaky voice. His long wet hair was stuck to his face and neck. His savage eyes bulged. "Some *thief* was trying to steal my collection!"

Deputy Rodney's car pulled up in front of our house. He jumped out of the vehicle.

"Take shelter *immediately*!" Deputy Rodney hollered through cupped hands. His uniform was soaked through to the skin.

Dad ignored him. He was still pawing through the pickup trucks. A giant tree fell across the street.

"Calvin, go to the root cellar!" Deputy Rodney ordered. "Take Benny. Now!"

"Either help me recover my stolen property," Dad raged, "or get the hell off my property!"

Deputy Rodney said a bad word. Then he unlocked the handcuffs on his belt.

"Benny," he yelled. "Crawl in the root cellar!"

"But there are *rats*!" I screamed.

"Then run down to the church hall basement!"

"But I can't—" I started to say.

Deputy Rodney was crying. "In the name of the law, Benny, do what I say. Run! Now!"

I ran as fast as I could. When I turned back to look, I saw Deputy Rodney pushing Dad into the backseat of the car.

Dad was in handcuffs.

CHAPTER 16

RAIN O'ER ME

MYRON WAS RUNNING TOWARD ME. "Come on," he yelled, leading me by the hand to the church hall. Trees were falling all around us.

We ran inside. I tried to pull the door closed behind us, but it didn't fit in the door frame. The building was already starting to twist out of shape.

"Never mind!" Myron said, pushing me toward the basement steps.

Just then the roof spun off like the lid of a jar.

"Don't look up!" Myron yelled.

But I couldn't help it. My eyes automatically swung up to see boards, shingles, and a black barbecue grill flying across the sky.

Myron and I tumbled down the steps. The basement was dark and wet and crammed full of people. Preacher Huffman held a flashlight.

"Stay under your tablecloths, please!" he said to the room.

Someone threw a small rug at Myron. It hit him in the face.

"Ow!" he said. "Oh, thanks. Here, Benny. Let's get under this."

The rug smelled like dirt, but we held it over our heads. A river of rain was pouring down the stairs. The noise overhead was deafening. Preacher Huffman was trying to get everyone to join him in the Our Father, but there were too many other competing conversations.

"It feels like we're on the *Titanic*!" someone yelled.

"It feels like a movie," someone else yelled.

"It feels like a tornado," a kid said, laughing. It sounded like one of the Ants brothers. It must've been one of the Ants brothers because he and his brothers started singing "Here Comes the Circus Train!"

"Where's the radio?" Myron asked the darkened room. "Mrs. Crumple, are you down here?"

"Yes, I'm here, Myron," she answered from across the room. "I have my radio, but I can't find 88.1 on the dial."

"Bet the antenna blew down," Myron said. "Don't worry. We're going to be okay. In fact . . ."

He listened for a second. Then for a few seconds more.

The rain was letting up. The hail had stopped. It was suddenly quiet.

Myron pulled the rug off our heads. Everyone was peeking out from under their tablecloths.

"Was that it?" Carmen asked.

"I think so," said Miss Tina Turnipson. "Thank goodness. It could've been a lot worse."

"It must've gone north," Mayor Prell said. He stood and moved so he could see up the staircase. "Replacing that roof will cost five grand, I bet."

"And we'll thank God if that's all the damage there is," Preacher Huffman said.

"That and a big mess," grumped Mrs. Verna Hartzell, folding up her tablecloth. "It's going to take a solid month to clean things up around here."

"We'll hire some help, Verna," Preacher Huffman assured her. "This is going to be more than we can tackle."

"You might think about getting some high school kids from Diamond," Mayor Prell said. "Don't let 'em up on the roof, but some hardworking kids could clean up better than—"

That's when we heard it. The deep, unmistakable howl that some people say sounds like a train. But I know what a train sounds like, and this was no train.

You hear it first in your ears, and then you feel it in your stomach, and then in your heart. And then you scream.

"Oh my God in heaven!" Carmen yelled.

"Cover your heads!" Preacher Huffman shouted.

"Aaaaaaaaaaaaaaaaaaaaaaah!"

For the next forty-five seconds, it was like we were in a blender. Everyone was thrown together and swirled and crushed and beaten. At first I thought we were being pelted by rain. But then I realized it was glass—tiny glass splinters—mixed in with the rain. Everything we were holding—tablecloths, rugs, a Christmas-tree skirt—was whipped out of our hands. The basement was no longer the basement because we could see the sky above us. But the sky didn't look like the sky because it was black. And then it was raining mud and wood and pieces of wall and more glass.

Every single person screamed. Most of us cried. My ears popped. Preacher Huffman kept reciting the Our Father while Carmen moaned, *"Dios mio! Dios mio! Dios mio!"*

"Verna isn't breathing!" someone hollered.

"We'll call an ambulance when we can!" someone yelled in response.

"Ooooooooooooooooh!" someone else yelled over the ear-splitting racket. It sounded like Chance. Or maybe Rance.

It was like we were all in the same car on the world's biggest roller coaster. It was like the scariest movie you've ever seen. It was like being in a wet cardboard box with someone throwing mud and broken glass at you.

For years to come, everyone would talk about what it was *like* because it was so hard to say what it *was*. It was all of those things, but it was more and worse and horrifying and really just impossible to describe in ordinary words. It was forty-five seconds of thinking you were dying, and hoping dying wouldn't hurt too much.

But what I'll never forget is the sound: the terrifying howl of that all-powerful sky. And all I could think of was that song Myron liked so much from *Quadrophenia*, "Love Reign O'er Me."

That's what the tornado sounded like. Like the loudest rock song in the world. Like someone screaming the word *LOOOOOOOOOVE* and then obliterating everything in sight.

CHAPTER 17

GET RIDE

THERE WAS NOTHING LEFT. Houses were shredded. Cars were crushed. Every tree in sight was mangled. It looked like someone had dropped a bomb on Dennis Acres.

"My restaurant!" Carmen cried.

"My house!" Miss Turnipson screamed.

"My piano!" Mrs. Crumple sobbed.

"Our town," Mayor Prell said sadly. "It's gone."

"Ringo," Myron whispered. "Ringo."

"My cats!" Mrs. Verna Hartzell shrieked. At least she was breathing again.

Dad, I thought. *Where is he?* Then I remembered the handcuffs. *Jail.*

I looked around for our house. All that was left was a messy mountain of shingles, broken glass, and big chunks of jagged boards. It was like someone had put our house through a wood chipper. It was trashed.

But the whole town was trashed now. Everything in Dennis Acres looked like our house.

"Every building in this town is toast," Mayor Prell said, as if reading my mind. "But at least we're alive. Thank God for that basement. I don't even want to think about anyone who was in a trailer."

Stormy.

I saw Dad's motorcycle lying in the middle of the street under a tangle of branches. I pulled it out. The mirrors fell off as soon as I stood the motorcycle up. It was dented all over, but the key was still in the ignition.

I climbed on the motorcycle and turned the key. Nothing. I tried to remember what Dad had done. I turned the key again and pulled in what I thought was the clutch. I flipped the foot lever out. I jumped up and quickly pushed down on the kick start. Nothing. I did it again. It started!

I lifted my foot for first gear. I let the clutch out as I twisted the accelerator toward me. I was moving. I was riding!

"Benny!" Myron yelled when he saw me. "Benny, no!"

But there was no time to explain. I had to think fast. I began to ride in a slow zigzag through the obstacle course in the street. It felt oddly familiar, like navigating through Dad's old junk piles in our house.

The only way I knew to get to Stormy's trailer was to take the school bus route. I started to ride toward Myron's shop to get my bearings. That would be my starting point.

But the shop was gone. Everything was gone. How had I forgotten that already? Sirens were wailing in the distance. I needed to think. *Think!*

I rode down the wet street until I got to the corner. I leaned right, taking it slow.

It's all about balance, Benny.

Just after I turned the corner, the motorcycle sputtered. I gave it more gas. The bike almost took off without me. The engine was running too fast. I knew I had to shift to a higher gear. I pulled in the clutch and pushed down on the left pedal. *There! Now I was riding!*

I had to slow down again when I got to the corner of Connecticut Avenue. The stop sign was torn off the post. I turned right and approached my first hill. I shifted into third gear to climb the hill. I was going fast, but I realized my mistake when I got to the top of the hill. A utility pole had fallen. The power line was drooping low across the street. I was riding too fast to stop. I didn't even have time to swerve. I just ducked my head and closed my eyes as I rode under the electric guillotine.

I turned left on 44th Street and saw a blue station wagon

turned upside down. A family was standing in a ditch. When they saw me, they pointed at their car. They were laughing and crying and hugging one another, all at the same time.

I turned right on Range Line Road and rode a mile before making a left on Saginaw Road. A farmer was standing in his field. He and his dairy cows looked wide-eyed and skittish, like they'd all just been through a car wash the wrong way.

Tractors and trucks were crumpled like tinfoil. Trees were twisted out of the ground, leaving their roots exposed. A round red barn I'd seen for years from the school bus window was blown to bits. A woman in an apron was running from a house, calling somebody's name. Maybe I should've stopped to see if she needed help, but I kept going.

I turned left on Highway V. Stormy's trailer was three miles away. Three miles of roller-coaster hills. I shifted from third gear to fourth and then into fifth. It felt like I was going a hundred miles an hour, but I didn't look down at the speedometer. I kept my eyes on the road. I'd ridden this route more than a thousand times, but I'd never been this close to the road before.

I'd never been in a tornado before.

I'd never ridden a motorcycle to Stormy's trailer before.

I was a mile away now. I gave the motorcycle more gas, but it was too much. I took a hill too fast. For a split second the bike left the road. When it landed, I felt the rear wheel slide sideways. I almost lost control.

It's all about balance, Benny.

I held the handlebars steady. I was almost there.

I passed the hog farm. Stormy's trailer was just ahead on the left. I made the turn. But when I pulled into her driveway, my heart stopped. There was nothing left except the cracked concrete slab where the trailer had once stood. My throat closed tight with tears.

"Benny! Benny!"

My head swiveled. It was Stormy, running toward me from the opposite direction. As she got closer, I saw a gash across her forehead.

"Stormy!" I said, jumping off the motorcycle. "You're bleeding. We have to—"

"Not me," she said, breathless. "My mom!"

Stormy led me down a hill to her mother, who was slumped over in the grass. Her face was streaked with blood.

"She got hit in the head by something," Stormy cried. "I think it was a wheelbarrow. She's bleeding bad, and I can't get her to wake up."

"We have to call an ambulance," I said. "Where can we call?"

"The trailer's gone!" Stormy said through tears.

"Maybe your neighbors—" I started to say.

"Everything's gone," she said, waving her arms frantically. "The phone lines are down. The power's gone." She started shaking her mother. "Mom, wake up! Wake up, Mom, please! *Please!*"

My mind was spinning. "We have to take her to a hospital," I said. "Do you think the two of us can get her on the motorcycle?"

"Yes!" Stormy said, choking on her tears. "I know we can."

I meant could we do it without killing her mom, but I didn't say that. I didn't want to upset Stormy any more than she already was. And besides, there was no alternative. We had to try.

I ran back to where I'd left the motorcycle and kick-started it. I rode it to a level spot near Stormy and her mom.

"Okay, here's the plan," I said, jumping off the bike. "We're going to lift your mom up here, okay? As gently as we can. Then you're going to sit behind her. I'm going to sit in front of her and drive."

"Okay," Stormy said. "Let's get her on this thing."

Stormy and I lifted her mom onto the motorcycle and propped her upright. Her eyes blinked open and closed.

"Mom?" Stormy said. "Mom? We're taking you to the hospital, okay? To see a doctor. Okay? Okay, Mom? Oh God, Benny. We have to hurry! We'll have to squeeze together really tight so she doesn't fall off."

Stormy climbed on behind her mom. I got on in front.

I was about to start the motorcycle when I remembered something.

"I don't know how to get to the hospital from here," I said over my shoulder.

"I do!" Stormy said quickly. "My mom used to work there. I know a shortcut down dirt roads. But wait, those roads sometimes flood. We better take the highway. Did you come down Highway V?"

"Yeah. I took the bus route."

"Okay. Go back that way until you get to Highway 71."

"Then what?"

"Turn right and go straight until I squeeze your arm. Whichever arm I squeeze, turn that direction."

So that's what we did. With her mother between us, Stormy held my arms just above the elbow as I rode back down Highway V. I took the hills slower this time. I squinted into the setting sun and concentrated on my passengers: One was barely conscious and the other had a history of getting carsick on hills.

As we approached the Highway 71 junction, I started to lean right.

"Hold on!" I hollered behind me.

"Whooooooooa," Stormy yelled as we made the sharp turn. She was squeezing both of my arms tightly.

"You okay?" I yelled over my shoulder. "Did I turn the wrong way?"

"Yes!" she called. "No! This is right! Keep going!"

"Okay!" I yelled back. It was almost like we were in Mrs. Rosso's class. "Can I borrow a piece of paper?"

"What?" Stormy yelled.

"Nothing!" I hollered into the wind. "I'll tell you later."

I wanted to make Stormy laugh, but it was a dumb joke. Nothing would make her laugh if her mom wasn't okay.

I needed to go faster. I shifted into fifth gear. Luckily, there weren't a lot of cars on the highway, but there were other things, weird things, like a big white birdcage and a patio umbrella turned inside out and the red hood of a car and a bashed-in hot water heater. I had to swerve to avoid hitting all of those, as well as a big brown sofa that was plopped like a bear in the middle of the highway. The crazy and hopeless assortment of stuff made me think of Dad. *How long will he be in jail? Will I be allowed to visit?*

Stormy started squeezing my left arm when we approached the exit for Highway 249. I made the turn. A half mile later when we came to Highway 44, Stormy squeezed my other arm.

Dad was right. It was all about balance. I was getting the hang of it. But I was freaking out about my dad and Stormy's mom. She felt lifeless behind me, like a sack of potatoes. What if she was already dead?

"Is she doing okay?" I yelled over my shoulder.

"I hope so," Stormy yelled back. "Keep going! We're more than halfway there!"

I tried to concentrate on the road in front of me, but I couldn't help noticing the trees on either side of the highway that had been pulled up by their roots like carrots. Telephone lines dangled loosely from their poles like Miss Turnipson's Mardi Gras necklaces.

Everything was like something else—carrots, necklaces, a sack of potatoes—because nothing felt real. It was like a dream. A dream that smelled like wet earth and mud. Like someone had just plowed a huge vegetable garden in the rain.

Stormy squeezed my right arm when we came to Exit 6. I knew we must be close because ambulances were speeding past us. I pulled over to the right lane to let them pass. Then I followed them to the emergency room entrance of St. John's Hospital.

When we arrived, Stormy's mom was conscious but groggy. A doctor and a nurse lifted her off the motorcycle and onto a bed with wheels. They pushed her inside the dark hospital. Stormy and I followed.

Broken glass was everywhere. Water was pouring out of burst pipes. Every lightbulb in the hospital had exploded. It was wet and dark and scary. But it was still a hospital—just a hospital that had taken a direct hit from a tornado.

A nurse took Stormy to a room to clean her bloody

forehead. I was waiting for her when I saw Deputy Rodney. He was walking down the dark hallway with a flashlight.

"Benny?" he said. "How did you know?"

"Know what?"

"That I brought your dad here," he said. "It was stupid to try to beat that twister. I could lose my job for that. But Benny?"

"Yeah?"

"Your dad's not well," Deputy Rodney said.

"I know."

"Maybe the doctors can help," he said.

"Really?" The thought had never occurred to me.

"They're giving him some medicine to help him sleep. You can visit him tomorrow. How bad is it in Dennis Acres?"

"Terrible," I said. "Everything's gone. Everything."

"Mmm," he said. "That's what I was afraid of. Here."

He gave me his flashlight. Then he wandered down the hall, swaying between walls. If I hadn't known better, I might've thought Deputy Rodney was drunk. But I knew better. We were all walking into walls that night.

Stormy found me a little while later. She had a white bandage covering her forehead. She was smiling.

"The nurse says my mom's going to be okay," she said. "She has a concussion, but it's not as bad as we thought."

"Great," I said. "That's really great."

"I know," Stormy said, laughing. She wiggled her arms and made a funny face. "My arms feel like they could fall off."

I'd forgotten that she'd held her mother in a protective hug all the way to the hospital.

"My dad's here, too," I said.

"Oh, no," Stormy said, dropping her arms. Her smile dissolved. "What happened to him?"

I shook my head. "I'm not sure."

She took my hands in hers. "The doctors here are good. Did you know I was born in this hospital during a power outage? My mom said they had to use candles in the delivery room."

"Really?" I asked.

"Yep."

Stormy and I wandered around the dark hospital for hours that night. Then we sat in the emergency room waiting area, watching all the people come in. I'd never seen so much blood in my life or heard words like *cardiac arrest* or *pneumothorax*. I'd never seen a man with a giant piece of glass sticking out of his back. I'd never seen a broken door used as a stretcher or a kid whose arms looked like bloody Shredded Wheat.

I held Stormy's hand when a woman ran through the doors screaming, "He's dead! He's dead! The car crushed him! What should I do?"

Nobody knew what to say—not even the doctors.

"It was so weird, Benny," Stormy said later that night. "The stuff that was flying through the air."

"I know," I said, remembering the barbecue grill I'd seen soaring over the church hall.

"I saw flying chickens and pigs," Stormy continued. "They must've been from the hog farm. But can you imagine—flying *pigs*?"

"Yeah."

Of course I could imagine flying pigs. Because how many times had I thought about the expression "when pigs fly"? A thousand times, at least. I'd always thought it meant never. Now I understood the expression was code for *anything could happen*. Anything was possible—from a tornado to a flying pig to a motorcycle ride with Stormy Walker.

CHAPTER 18

JUST SPLINTERS

STORMY AND I STAYED with Mrs. Rosso in Diamond that night. Stormy knew where she lived from trick-or-treating. Deputy Rodney gave us a ride. He suggested I leave the motorcycle at the hospital.

Mrs. Rosso hugged us so hard I thought she was going to break my ribs. She ran a bath for Stormy in her tub and told me to take a shower in the guest room. She laid out clean clothes for us: gym shorts and a University of Minnesota sweatshirt for Stormy, a light blue jogging suit for me. I was too tired to be embarrassed.

Mrs. Rosso had been decorating bulletin boards at school when the tornado hit.

"You know how you always hear stories about people

riding out tornadoes in their bathtub?" she said. "Well, that's what I did. I didn't have time to go to the basement of the school. So I just climbed in that old claw-foot tub and buried myself in pillows."

We were in her kitchen. She was making us grilled peanut-butter sandwiches. The roof was leaking a little, but other than that, her house was fine.

"What's school look like?" Stormy asked.

"Not so good," Mrs. Rosso said, licking the knife. "But hey, maybe we can finish out the year in a tent. That'd be fun, wouldn't it? I wonder if I could rent a tent big enough for our whole class."

Mrs. Rosso could make anything seem fun.

The next morning I asked her to call Myron and tell him I was okay.

"Myron?" she asked.

"He's my friend," I said. "Really he's my dad's friend, but he's my friend, too."

"Honey," said Mrs. Rosso, stirring pancake batter, "I don't think there's anywhere left to call in Dennis Acres."

"Can we drive over to check?" I asked. "Please?"

"We can't visit our parents until eleven o'clock," Stormy said. "A nurse told me. We could check on Benny's friend before we go to the hospital."

Mrs. Rosso cried quietly on the drive to Dennis Acres. I stared out the car window. A few roofless houses remained.

The trees that survived were all stripped bare of their leaves and small limbs. They looked like witches' hands. Somehow the devastation seemed more real a day later. But I knew what Stormy meant when she said it looked like a bad dream.

"It's like a big mean giant just stomped through here in his boots," she said, staring out her side of the car.

We found Myron with a chain saw. He was carving up two trees that had fallen on one-armed Dallas Emery's truck.

"Benny!" Myron said, dropping the chain saw when he saw me. "Benny!"

His glasses were gone and he had dark circles under his eyes. His clothes were still covered in mud from the tornado. We hugged and laughed. Then he slung his arm around my shoulder.

I introduced Myron to Stormy and Mrs. Rosso. They were talking when I saw Ringo galloping toward us.

"Ringo!" I cried.

"Can you believe it?" Myron asked. "Not a scratch on him. And guess who saved Mrs. Hartzell's cats?"

"Who?" I asked.

Myron kissed Ringo's fur. "This guy right here. He carried those cats one by one out of the rubble by the scruff of their necks."

"What a good dog," Mrs. Rosso said, rumpling Ringo's ears. She spoke softly to Myron. "Did you lose anyone?"

"No," Myron replied. "We're all okay here. How about you?"

"I'm fine," she said. "I was lucky. But other places are . . ." She shook her head. "There's nothing left."

"Splinters," Myron replied gravely. "Just splinters."

I could tell from his face what he was thinking. I was thinking the same thing.

"Where's your dad?" he asked.

"The hospital," I said.

Myron looked confused.

"We're going that way now," Mrs. Rosso said. "Do you want to come with us?"

Mrs. Rosso and Stormy went to visit her mom while Myron and I tried to find Dad. It took us a while to track him down. The lady at the front desk said they were still trying to sort out all the new patients who had been admitted after the tornado.

"What's the nature of Mr. Summer's injury?" she asked. Her fingers were flipping through pages on a clipboard. "Trauma? Heart attack? Broken bone? Just give me an idea so I know what I'm looking for."

I turned to Myron for help.

"Uh, it's a little complicated," Myron told the lady. "Never mind. We'll find him."

When we finally did find Dad on the psychiatric floor, two doctors were in the room with him.

"Hey!" Dad said when he saw us. "Docs, this is my son, Benny, and my best friend, Myron."

Dad looked clean and comfortable. Someone had washed his hair. I checked his wrists. No handcuffs.

"The doctors here were just telling me about my brain," Dad said, grinning widely. "They want to do some experiments on me."

"A clinical trial," one of the doctors said, smiling. "There are some promising new drugs in development. Selective serotonin reuptake inhibitors."

"You know what serotonin is, don't you, Myron?" Dad said excitedly. "It's a neurotransmitter. Electrochemical communication between neurons takes place all the time in the brain." He turned to the doctors. "I think I get this, you guys. I really do. The brain is like a computer, right?"

"That's right," the second doctor said. "Mr. Summer, we'll need to be able to count on you to take the prescribed dosage every day. And you'll have to come in for evaluations and cognitive behavior therapy."

"No problem," Dad said. "Benny can keep track of all the pills and appointments. He's good at that kind of thing."

"We want *you* to be good at that kind of thing, too," said the smiling doctor. "That's the whole idea. We're told things had gotten a little out of hand at your house."

"Yeah, I guess you could say that," Dad said casually,

raking his hands through his clean hair. "It was getting a little thick in there."

Thick? My eyes nearly popped out of my head.

Myron signaled the doctors with his head. They walked out in the hallway to talk.

"How you doing, Benny?" Dad asked when we were alone.

"Okay," I said.

"Good," he said, closing his eyes. "That's good."

I didn't know if he was sleeping or just resting. It'd been a long time since Dad had slept in a bed. It must've felt nice after sleeping for months on a sofa piled high with mail and computer magazines.

I knew I should let him rest. But I had to tell him. I just had to.

"Dad?" I said.

"Yeah," he answered, not opening his eyes.

"Remember what you said about your holy splinter? The true splinter from the Holy Cross?"

"Mmm-hmm," he murmured.

"Remember how you said you wouldn't get rid of it until pigs flew?"

He opened his eyes and frowned. "Yeah?"

"Well, guess what? Pigs flew last night in the tornado. My friend saw them. Pigs were flying through the air. Can you believe it?"

He looked at me. Then he smiled and closed his eyes.

"Cool," he said softly, his lips curling into the old familiar smirk.

"You're not upset?" I asked.

"Nah," he said, his eyes still closed. "I lost it a long time ago."

"*What?*"

"New Orleans," Dad said. "Nineteen-seventy. The day after Mardi Gras. I lost it. The splinter from the Holy Cross."

That's when my eyes really did pop out of my head.

"I *got* a splinter," I said, zooming my index finger within an inch of his closed eyes. "It was from a wooden Mardi Gras mask."

My mind was whirling. I took a breath and kept talking, even faster.

"I crossed my finger, *this* finger, when it was still sore from the splinter, over Miss Turnipson's fingers. It was right before she mailed the application to America's Most Charming Small Town Contest. It couldn't be the same splinter, could it? Could it, Dad? And these were the same fingers I used to play 'Für Elise' on the piano. I mean, I kinda played it and I kinda didn't. But it was right before the tornado. Before pigs flew. Hey Dad, do you think Mom will come home now?"

But he was sleeping. His face, now at rest, no longer wore a smirk but a look of deep, unrelenting sadness. It was the face of a nineteen-year-old boy who had once tried to impress a girl with his most valuable treasure. And then he'd lost it.

"Dad?" I said again. "Dad?"

"It's not a toy, Calvin," he whispered in his sleep. "Whatever you do, don't lose it. It's from the Holy Cross."

* * *

Stormy and I stayed at Mrs. Rosso's house again that night. We drank milkshakes and ate M&M's while we worked on a five-hundred-piece puzzle of a castle in the clouds reflected in water.

"You know," Stormy said, easily piecing together the drawbridge to the castle, "you saved my mom's life."

"I don't know about that," I said. I was getting nowhere on the turrets.

"I do," Stormy insisted. "If you hadn't taken us to the hospital, my mom could've died." She popped an M&M in her mouth.

I knew it wasn't that simple.

"But I never would've learned how to ride the motorcycle if Mrs. Rosso hadn't assigned the service project," I explained. "And I wouldn't have thought about doing a service project at home if you hadn't given me the idea first—or if Dad hadn't yelled at Mrs. Rosso on the phone. Of course it was Dad's motorcycle, but he never would've built it if it hadn't been for Myron's séance."

I stopped to shovel a handful of M&M's in my mouth.

"But," I said, chewing, "Dad never would've had the

Ouija board for the séance if he'd thrown away all his junk like Mom wanted him to. When you stop to think about it, it's all pretty tangled up and complicated."

I considered telling Stormy about Dad's splinter, but it seemed too crazy to mention. I didn't want her to think I was nuts. And it's not like the splinter had been triple lucky or even single lucky. Anyone looking at Dennis Acres that night could've seen that.

"We might never get connected to the world's giant computer network," I said instead. "But our small-town network is pretty cool."

Stormy was staring at me like I was a five-hundred-piece puzzle in the clouds reflected in water.

"I don't know what the heck you're talking about," she said. "But you saved my mom's life, whether you want to believe it or not."

Truth is, I did believe it, but I thought it'd seem like bragging to say so. And I didn't want to brag to Stormy. I wanted her to like me.

CHAPTER 19

GIVEN THE CIRCUMSTANCES

SO IF I WAS SUCH A BIG LIFESAVER, why couldn't I save my parents' marriage? Easy. Because my mom and dad didn't get along.

Mom arrived in Dennis Acres two days after pigs flew in the tornado. She was like a tornado herself.

"For the love of God, I can't *believe* your father wasn't with you during the tornado," she fumed. "Benny, you could've *died*! You could've been sucked up inside that twister and blown to kingdom come. You could've been torn to shreds, bit by bit, bone by bone, with blood coming out your eyes and ears and nose."

"Mom, I'm fine," I said.

"I know," she replied, waving one hand in the air. "But that's why I've got to take you back to Louisiana. There are no tornadoes there."

"There are hurricanes," I pointed out.

"Not the same thing," she said. "You know when they're coming. Hurricanes don't sneak up on you out of nowhere and *wham!*" She slammed her fist into her opposite hand. "Knock you senseless."

I felt like I was being knocked senseless by this conversation.

"You'll love Louisiana," she insisted. "The food, the music, the people. There's no winter, no snakes. Okay, sure, maybe an alligator or two in the bayou. And big giant cockroaches the size of mice, but we can spray for those. It'll be home. Just you and me."

"It wouldn't be the same," I said quietly. "I don't want to leave Dennis Acres."

She put her face right up to mine. "Benny, look at me. There's never been one good thing about Dennis Acres. Not one thing. And now there's *nothing*. Nothing! There's nothing to leave because there's nothing *here* anymore. Don't you get that?"

I did. But I also knew my homesickness would get worse if I left. I still thought of it as homesickness back then. I didn't know what else to call the heavy ache inside that made me feel unredeemable.

Later that day Miss Tina Turnipson thumbtacked a poster

on a bulletin board outside Myron's former shop. After the tornado, the old bulletin board I'd tried to throw away became the communications hub of Dennis Acres. The poster said: REPRESENTATIVES FROM THE U.S. CHAMBER OF COMMERCE SEND THEIR DEEPEST SYMPATHIES FOR OUR LOSSES AND BEST WISHES FOR OUR RECOVERY. THEY WILL NOT BE HERE TODAY AS PLANNED.

Before the day was over, someone had scrawled "Figures" across the poster.

But a week later another poster appeared on the bulletin board. This one said: IMPORTANT! REPRESENTATIVES FROM THE U.S. CHAMBER OF COMMERCE WILL BE HERE ON MAY 20TH TO MAKE AN IMPORTANT ANNOUNCEMENT. MEET HERE AT 1 P.M.

A construction crew arrived two days later and built a plywood platform with steps on two sides. Chairs arrived the next day followed by a microphone stand, a theater-style screen, and a flagpole.

For everyone still picking through the piles of tornado debris, looking for treasures to salvage, it was frustrating to see all the work being put into a temporary stage. But it was something to look forward to, and we all needed that, especially after camping out in the Red Cross shelters set up in nearby schools and churches.

May twentieth fell on a Friday. Like dutiful sheep, we gathered in front of the stage shortly before one o'clock.

"They're not here," Carmen grumbled. "I bet they're not coming."

"Why do they have to come here in person to tell us we don't get the new calculators?" one-armed Dallas Emery complained. "Why'nt they just write us a letter?"

"Because we don't have a post office anymore," Izzy answered unpleasantly.

"They're *coming*," Miss Turnipson promised mysteriously. "Their plane flew into Springfield this morning. I'm sure they're driving over right now."

"Hmpf," Mrs. Verna Hartzell snorted.

But Miss Turnipson was right. At five minutes before one, a shiny black Cadillac glided into Dennis Acres. Because of all the tornado debris, the car had to park several blocks away from the stage area.

A trio of men in blue suits, white shirts, and red ties strode toward us. They smiled as they ascended the stage. Only one man spoke. His name was Mr. Bob Johnson.

"I am here today on behalf of the U.S. Chamber of Commerce and its member affiliates across this great nation to extend our sympathies for your recent losses," Mr. Bob Johnson began. "Not only do we mourn the loss of the place you call home, we also mourn the loss of America's Most Charming Small Town."

"Oh, puh-lease," Mom groaned.

"Shhhhhh," Miss Turnipson hissed. "Listen!"

"Given the circumstances," Mr. Bob Johnson continued, "we hope you can understand why we no longer feel it's appropriate to give a personal computer to every household in Dennis Acres."

"Saw that coming a mile away," Mr. Dallas Emery muttered in a voice loud enough for everyone to hear. He turned to leave.

Mr. Bob Johnson stepped closer to the microphone. "We'd like to give every household a new *home* instead."

Everyone froze. Mouths hung wide open.

"That's right," Mr. Bob Johnson said. "We plan to bring in construction crews from all over the country to rebuild the picturesque town of Dennis Acres with its charming thatched cottages and English country gardens."

I looked at Myron. He was looking at Miss Turnipson. She was staring at her shoes and nibbling her bottom lip like a rabbit.

"We're going to rebuild it just like it was before," Mr. Bob Johnson said, "beginning with the lovely fountain on the town square."

"Fountain?" Preacher Huffman whispered.

"Town square?" Mayor Roland Prell asked.

"We feel," Mr. Bob Johnson said, his voice rising dramatically, "that we should honor the spirit of Dennis Dennison, who in 1879 donated his private peacock ranch to his friends and neighbors so that this remarkable town could be born."

"Dennis Dennison?" Myron mouthed the words to Miss Turnipson. "Peacock ranch?"

"Creative writing," Miss Turnipson whispered back. "I made it up for the contest. Shh."

"Of course," continued Mr. Bob Johnson, "to truly replicate the spirit and architectural integrity of your charming town, we will welcome any historical photos you have of Dennis Acres so that we—"

"All destroyed!" Myron yelled between cupped hands. "The tornado destroyed all photos of Dennis Acres." He gave Miss Turnipson a fiendish wink.

"In that case," said Mr. Bob Johnson, "we will rely on this lovely picture by Miss Tina Turnipson."

He pushed a button and unfurled on the screen behind him a huge reproduction of Miss Turnipson's pen-and-ink drawing.

"Oh!" Mrs. Verna Hartzell said, her elderly eyes gleaming at the sight. "Will you look at that?"

"Ahhhh!" sang Carmen. "It's beautiful."

"Looks like the insides on one of them Christmas snow globes," Mr. Dallas Emery chimed in.

"We at the U.S. Chamber of Commerce can't wait to restore Dennis Acres to its rightful glory," Mr. Bob Johnson said with authority. "We hope to have new homes built for everyone within a year."

"What about my restaurant?" asked Carmen. "It's the

only restaurant in town and the best business, too. We need good businesses in Dennis Acres so we have jobs for our people."

"Couldn't agree more," Mr. Bob Johnson said. "We'll be happy to rebuild your restaurant."

"Will the post office be rebuilt?" Izzy asked.

"And the church?" added Preacher Huffman.

"Yes and yes," said Mr. Bob Johnson with a satisfied laugh. "We're going to rebuild *everything* just as it was in the drawing Miss Turnipson submitted with her entry in the competition for America's Most Charming Small Town."

I saw Miss Turnipson's eyes dart in Myron's direction. Now he was looking at his feet and kicking dirt.

"Excuse me, Mr. Johnson," Miss Turnipson said in a clear voice. "There were a few things I *didn't* include in my drawing for reasons of space and, uh, artistic composition. But please understand, sir, that Dennis Acres wouldn't be Dennis Acres without Myron Kazie's electronics shop or his radio station, KZ88."

Mr. Bob Johnson pointed at the men in suits. "Add that to the list. In fact, we better rebuild the radio station first so you have a reliable source of information during the coming year. We'll make it a state-of-the-art radio station and add a generator backup, too."

Myron laughed and ruffled Ringo's fur. "Did you hear that, Ringo? A brand-new station." Then he hollered up to

Mr. Bob Johnson. "Please don't forget our friends who lost their homes on the outskirts of town!"

"We won't!" Mr. Bob Johnson hollered back generously.

"Don't forget my cats!" Mrs. Verna Hartzell suddenly remembered. "They had their own house before the tornado. They should get their own house after the tornado."

Mr. Bob Johnson frowned and looked at the two men in suits. The two men looked at each other. One whispered something to the other. The other whispered something back. They turned to Mr. Bob Johnson and shrugged.

"It would be our pleasure, ma'am," Mr. Bob Johnson said.

"Thank you," Mrs. Hartzell said, her lips forming a pickled smile. "You can keep your calculators. We just need some new houses around here."

"And a fountain!" yelled Mr. Dallas Emery triumphantly. "Don't forget our fountain! You boys build it just like Tina Turnipson drew it. That gal knows what she's doing." He turned and gave Miss Turnipson a jaunty thumbs-up. It was the one-armed man's noblest gesture.

Miss Turnipson smiled in return. When she saw the stunned expression on my face, she elbowed her way through the crowd till she was standing next to me.

"The worldwide computer nougat isn't ready yet," she whispered in my ear.

"I know," I whispered back. I remembered the conversation I'd overheard between Mom and Dad months earlier; the fight about the holy splinter and the giant computer network that was coming to connect everyone in the whole wide world.

Miss Turnipson was beaming. "The Chamber of Commerce suggested building new homes for everyone instead," she chirped. "Isn't it so *lucky*?" She crossed her fingers and held them up above her head. "Triple lucky," she said, waving her hand in the afternoon sun.

I crossed my two fingers in solidarity. Then I turned my hand around and looked closely at my index finger.

The splinter was long gone. Of course it was.

* * *

That night I ate dinner in the hospital cafeteria with Mom, Myron, Mrs. Rosso, and Stormy. Mrs. Rosso laughed and clapped her hands when she heard the plans for Dennis Acres.

"Unbelievable," she said, shaking her head. "A dream come true."

"You're right!" Myron agreed, roaring at the hilarity of it all. "That's exactly what it is."

"I guess if you like living in Dennis Acres, it is," Mom moped. She'd been home less than two weeks, but already a storm was brewing inside her. Mom's bad mood was due to a combination of sleeping in a Red Cross shelter at night and taking me to see Dad in the hospital every day. The doctors asked her to stay in the cafeteria after her first and only visit with Dad woke up every patient on the floor.

"I'll tell you right now," Mom continued, "you can build all the fountains you want in Dennis Acres, but it'll never be New Orleans. Carmen makes the worst coffee I've ever tasted. You can't get good coffee in Missouri—or beignets. You know what a beignet is, don't you?"

"Let's go see what kind of ice cream they have," I said to Stormy, pulling her up by the arm as the adult conversation veered dangerously close to the source of my name.

"Ice cream?" she asked.

"You scream," I answered.

"We *both* screamed," she corrected with a laugh.

And she was right. We both had screamed on the night of the tornado. But something else had happened that night, too. In the middle of all the awfulness, we had found something wonderful and lucky: each other.

Still, I didn't want Stormy to hear my mom explain what a beignet was. I was certain I'd die of humiliation if the only girl I'd ever liked found out I was named after a deep-fried powdered sugar donut.

CHAPTER 20

WELCOME TO BEIGNET ACRES

TURNS OUT I WAS WRONG. I didn't die when Stormy found out about my name. I didn't die when the whole town found out about my name. I didn't even die when my mom had a professional sign made that said WELCOME TO BEIGNET ACRES, HOME OF THE BEST BEIGNETS AND COFFEE NORTH OF NEW ORLEANS. The bottom of the sign had a picture of me and the words MAKE IT A BEIGNET SUMMER!

She propped the sign in front of a card table she set up every morning beginning in June. That's when two hundred construction workers descended upon Dennis Acres to start the rebuilding effort. Every morning my mom was outside making beignets in a deep fryer connected to a propane tank. And every morning two hundred construction workers bought at least one order of fried donuts and one cup of Mom's coffee. Most came back for seconds.

Mom's beignet stand was so successful, Carmen asked Mom if she wanted to go into business together.

"You make beignets and coffee for breakfast, and I'll make fish tacos and lemonade for lunch," Carmen suggested. "We'll make a killing. And when my restaurant reopens, you can make your beignets in the morning there. I've never been open for breakfast before."

Mom was flattered by the idea. She and Carmen got along like chips and salsa. But the idea of staying in Dennis Acres only made Mom cranky. She said she was just making hay while the sun shined, and that as soon as her divorce was final, she was leaving Dennis Acres. For good. With me.

When Dad got out of the hospital, he moved into the motel on Highway 44 where all of us lived while Dennis Acres was being rebuilt. The Chamber of Commerce paid for one motel room for every household. Mom got a good deal on her own room in exchange for vacuuming the motel hallways every night. I divided my time equally between the two rooms.

Mom and Dad went to see a lawyer in June to get a divorce. In August I had to go with them to the courthouse in Neosho. The judge wanted to talk to all of us together.

"Nola Rene Summer," the judge began, looking at a piece of paper. "Tell the court why you're requesting sole custody of your son."

"Because I'm his mother," Mom said crisply from under her helmet of curling-ironed hair. "And because I can give him a better life in Louisiana than his father could ever hope to give him in Dennis Acres."

"Calvin Eugene Summer," the judge said, "why are you requesting sole custody of your son?"

"'Cause Dennis Acres is Benny's home," Dad said. "It's the only home he's ever known. And because Nola abandoned Benny. She left him in the middle of the night. A good mother would never throw away her own child."

The judge stared at Mom and Dad. Then he looked at me.

"Who do you want to live with, Beignet? Your mom or your dad?"

"Both?" I said.

The judge ordered shared custody on the condition that Mom stay in Missouri until I was eighteen, and that Dad keep his motel room clean and also his new house, when it was built.

"Judge, with all due respect, that is insulting and unfair," Mom said. She was wearing a new dress for her court appearance. "And besides, it's completely unrealistic to think that Calvin will *ever* be able to keep a clean house. He's been a pack rat since the day we got married. Even in a brand-new house, he'll fill it with crap. Piles of crap, I'm telling you, he *will*."

The judge took a deep breath before responding. "With all due respect to you, madam, I'm looking at a report here from Mr. Summer's doctors. They believe with proper therapy, treatment, and considerable effort on his part, Calvin can learn to control his desire to fill his living environment with . . . an excessive amount of things."

I thought Mom was going to explode. "But, don't you *understand*? Calvin is demented! He's sick in the head! It runs on his side of the family. He gets it from his grandmother. They're all crazy, but especially Calvin. He's *crazy*."

"Maybe," said the judge slowly. "But as my Irish grandmother used to say, we're all a wee bit mad on one subject or the other."

I wondered what subject I was a wee bit mad about. Probably something about my mom and dad. Probably my crazy wish that they could ever get along.

Mom wasn't giving up. "Judge, you're not listen—"

"In cases like these," the judge said, rolling right over her, "I like to wait and watch."

"Wait and watch?" Dad asked. He was wearing his lucky *Star Trek* T-shirt, freshly washed for the occasion.

"Wait and watch," the judge repeated.

"Hrmpf," Mom said, crossing her arms stiffly. "I guess we could give it a try."

"That's the spirit," said the judge. "I'd like to see you all back here in ninety days to hear how it's going. In the meantime, I'll talk to the Chamber of Commerce fellas about building two houses for the Summer family."

"Wait," said Dad. "I have to keep *two* houses clean?"

"No," the judge said, a smile passing quickly over his face. "Just one. You'll have one house. Your ex-wife will have the other. Your son will divide his time between the two houses in a way the court deems most beneficial to him. Is that agreeable to you, Beignet?"

"Yes," I said. "Thank you."

Dad didn't discuss the divorce much with me. He just said his marriage to Mom belonged in the unredeemable box.

Mom was more talkative. She said she didn't hate Dad, but she didn't love him the way a wife should love a husband. That's when she was feeling charitable. When she was in her Hurricane Nola mood, she said Dad was nuts.

"But as long as I don't have to live with him," she said, "I don't care what he does."

I did have to live with Dad. Part of the time, anyway. I can't say I always liked it, but I can say that I always wanted Dad to get better. So I made sure he took the pills the doctors gave him and went to every appointment.

After the tornado, Dad lost interest in connecting to the world's biggest computer network. He said after reading about the brain, he was more interested in building a computer small enough to hold in your hand.

"I'm going to build the world's smallest computer," he told me one day that summer. "It's going to be a tiny computer that's also a telephone, a calculator, a stereo, a phone answering service, a camera, a slide carousel for pictures, a talking compass, and a phone book, white pages and yellow." He was laughing. "I know I can do this, Benny. I know it. Just wait and watch. Wait and watch. It's going to be small enough to hold in your hand or fit in your pocket. No cords, no wires. None of that clutter that just gets in the way. Oh, and I'm also going to add a digital bulletin board so people can send you messages anytime from any place in the whole wide world."

Poor Dad, I said to myself a million times that summer. I wondered what would ever become of him.

Myron gave Dad a private workroom at his new electronics shop. Myron also gave me my own radio show. You can probably guess who I asked to be my first guest.

CHAPTER 21

THE FIRST INTERVIEW (LOVE REIGN O'ER EVERYBODY)

MYRON DECIDED MY RADIO SHOW should be on Friday afternoons between four and five o'clock.

"Because that's the magic hour for teenagers," he said.

It was October. We were sitting in Myron's new radio studio surrounded by shiny new microphones, turntables, and cassette tape decks. Ringo was sleeping under the console. An old-fashioned school clock hung on the wall. Myron said he didn't trust a clock that didn't have hands.

"Magic hour?" I said. "What're you talking about?"

"Friday afternoons," Myron explained. "You're young, you have the whole weekend in front of you, maybe there's a girl you're interested in. You'll see."

"I'm only *twelve*," I reminded him. Sometimes I think

Myron forgot this. "I won't be thirteen until November twelfth."

He laughed. "Nothing wrong with thinking ahead. And hey, one of these days I've got to teach you how to make mix tapes. They'll be handy when you start dating. Start with Burt Bacharach. Add a little Motown. Then Zeppelin. You've got to have Led Zeppelin. Then maybe add Pete Townshend singing 'Heart to Hang Onto.' Or, 'See Me, Feel Me, Touch Me, Heal Me.' Or, if you want something more upbeat, you could go with 'Let My Love Open the Door.'"

"Myron, stop, please," I begged because I could hear Stormy and Mrs. Rosso in the front room. Stormy had agreed to be my first guest. Mrs. Rosso wanted to take pictures.

I asked Myron to transcribe the interview. When I went back later to read the transcript, I saw he'd quit halfway through. This is all he had.

TRANSCRIPT
Benny's first show: 10/6/1983

BENNY: Hi, this is Benny Summer. Thanks for tuning in. This is my first show, so please forgive any mistakes or goofs. I'm still getting the hang of things here. The new equipment's pretty fancy. We have five phone lines now, a bigger antenna, and a

stronger transmitter. So if you're listening at the motel and want to call in, you
know the number. Same as before. 555-6804.
Now, um . . . uh . . . er . . .

MRS. ROSSO: (whispering) You're doing
great, Benny.

MYRON: Introduce your guest.

BENNY: Oh, yeah. Thanks. I know everyone
will enjoy meeting my guest today. Her
name is Stormy Walker. Hey, Stormy.

STORMY: Hey, Benny.

BENNY: Thanks for coming in. My first
question for you is something I've always
wondered. How'd you get your name? I'm
guessing there's a story behind it.

STORMY: You guessed right. I was born on a
stormy night. May 5, 1971. There was a
tornado in Joplin. My mom barely made it
to the hospital.

BENNY: Really? I didn't know there was a tornado in 1971. Oh, looks like we have a phone call. Let's see if this works. Hello?

TINA TURNIPSON: Hi, it's Miss Turnipson. Speaking of names, do you know how Dennis Acres got its name?

BENNY: No, but something tells me it doesn't have anything to do with a peacock ranch, right?

TINA TURNIPSON: (Laughs) Maybe not. But I checked with a research librarian in Joplin. There's no definitive history on how Dennis Acres got its name. So I can make up any story I like.

BENNY: Yes, you can, Miss Turnipson. And Mrs. Rosso will remind you that it's fiction. Looks like we have another call. Hello?

MRS. CRUMPLE: I'm calling to find out when you're coming for your first piano lesson.

BENNY: Oh. Hi, Mrs. Crumple. I sorta forgot about that.

MRS. CRUMPLE: I noticed. I'm making my summer schedule. My new house will be ready by then. You can come for lessons on Wednesdays at four o'clock.

BENNY: Really? Can't I . . . um . . . dang.

STORMY: You're lucky, Benny. I've always wanted to take piano lessons.

MYRON: Why don't you two take lessons together? Mrs. Crumple, would that be okay? Maybe you could teach Benny and Stormy some duets.

MRS. CRUMPLE: Fine with me.

BENNY: Myron, why don't you take guitar lessons? As much as you like listening to music, you should learn how to play some songs on the guitar.

MYRON: Huh. I never thought about that. I don't suppose you could give me guitar lessons, could you, Mrs. Crumple?

MRS. CRUMPLE: Of course. Music is music. Come on Wednesdays after the kids.

(Myron started asking a lot of questions here about acoustic versus electric guitars, and which he should start with, and whether or not he'd be expected to play in the annual recital. He was too busy talking to write. He started transcribing again near the end of the hour.)

STORMY: We only have a minute or so left, and we haven't talked about your name yet, Benny. You never told me your real name was Beignet.

BENNY: I wonder why.

STORMY: Well, I think it's the perfect name for you because beignets are from Louisiana, like your mom. But they're sorta different, like your dad. And you're different, Benny. You really are different.

This is where Myron stopped transcribing. He was probably too busy laughing to write. I remember that I squirmed in my chair and looked at the clock. One minute left till the top of the hour. Stormy was still talking about my name.

"But most of all, your names fits you because you're sweet," Stormy said. "Like a donut with powdered sugar on top."

I groaned and looked to Myron for help.

"She's got you there, Ben," he said. When other people started calling me Beignet, Myron began calling me Ben. A definite improvement.

"But you *are* sweet," Stormy insisted. "Even my mom thinks you're sweet. She got a job making beignets with your mom at Carmen's Casita because of you."

"Well, that's good," I said quickly, trying to change the subject. "I think your mom will really—"

"Benny," Stormy interrupted, "don't you know you're the sweetest boy in the whole school?"

Jeez Louise. I think I might've even said that out loud.

I looked at Mrs. Rosso. She just smiled and kept snapping the pictures she would give me years later in a photo album when I graduated from college. In return I would write this book for her. For her and for Myron. It was my gift to them when they got married.

But on that Friday afternoon, I just looked at the clock. Only forty-five seconds left in my first interview.

"I'm sweet?" I said. "C'mon. Myron, help me out here."

He shrugged and leaned back in his chair, his hands locked behind his head.

"Never argue with someone who thinks you're cool," he said, grinning.

His advice made me think about Mom and Dad. Was there ever a time they thought the other person was cool? There must've been. I just wasn't there to see it.

That made me think about the past and all the things I hadn't seen. I thought about Social Studies and the year 1789 with the Bill of Rights and the French Revolution. Was history just one long story of people trying to get along?

Then I thought about the tornado that roared through Dennis Acres and how it sounded like it was screaming LOOOOOOOOOVE before it turned everything to splinters.

But there we were in Myron's new radio studio. We'd survived it. We would go on, all of us: Myron, Mrs. Rosso, Stormy, me. Mom and Dad, too, not together, but separately. Miss Tina Turnipson, one-armed Dallas Emery, Mrs. Crumple, the Ants brothers (they weren't so bad), Mrs. Hartzell, her cats, and good old Ringo.

And Dad's mysterious splinter, wherever it was. Maybe it was nowhere. Maybe it was everywhere.

And Stormy liked me.

Of course I liked her, too, even though I couldn't tell her

that. But sitting there that day, I could imagine a time when I would be able to tell a girl I liked her—and more.

It took ten more years before I was brave enough to say "I love you" to someone, and when I did it wasn't to Stormy. But she was a lot like Stormy, and the reason I could say it to her was because I'd felt it on that day in that room with those people.

It wasn't a rock 'n' roll guitar-smashing *LOVE* scream, but a soft voice in my heart that felt gentle and true and like the opposite of homesickness. It was love. *Love*.

And because I couldn't say that word on that fall afternoon as the hands on the clock moved so effortlessly from one magic hour to the next, I said two other words instead.

"Thank you," I whispered. And then I said it again louder. *"Thank you."*

MY THANKS

To Liz Szabla, not only for her endless editorial wisdom and friendship, but also for encouraging me to write this story. I am triple lucky to have met Liz.

To Myron Jackson, Kazie Perkins, and Chris "Music Soup" Hartzell at KZGM 88.1 FM in Cabool, Missouri. It really is the friendliest little community radio station you'd ever want to listen to.

To my pals at the Joplin Public Library, especially Jeana Gockley, who gave me my first tour of Joplin after the tornado, along with a map of Dennis Acres, which is, in fact, a tiny unincorporated neighborhood on the south side of Joplin. I'm happy to report that Dennis Acres was unharmed by the 2011 twister.

To Tim Bryant, for the primer on motorcycles and the margin notes, and for helping me clean out a barn only Calvin Summer could love.

To April Rosso at Norwood Elementary School, for being everybody's favorite librarian and my heaven-sent technology tutor.

To Phil O'Brien, for thirty years of good music, beginning with his radio show, *The Night Owl Presents,* on the Marquette University radio station.

To Laura Biagi, for introducing me to the genius of Pete Townshend back in 1983 when we were still listening to cassette tapes and clacking away on electric typewriters.

And a belated thanks to my late grandmother, Mary Shaw Klise, for giving my dad an alleged true splinter from the Holy Cross. Thanks, too, to Dad, for losing that splinter in the chaos of our Moss Avenue house so that I could spend all these years wondering where in the world it was, and if it could possibly be real.

Go Fish!

KATE KLISE

© Dawn Shields

You've mentioned before that an image is usually the first thing you think of when starting to write a book. What image did you start with for *Homesick*?

I began this one with the image of the holy splinter. Believe it or not, my grandmother really *did* give my dad a splinter she claimed was from the crucifix. My dad promptly lost it. I have vivid memories of searching for that splinter as a child, wondering if there was any chance it could be real.

Have you ever seen or experienced a tornado?

I've spent much of my life in the Midwest, where tornadoes are common. I've taken cover in basements and in closets dozens of times, but thank goodness, I've never seen or suffered a tornado. I have covered the aftermath, though, when I was a reporter for *People* magazine. I also spent more than a decade working as a freelance disaster writer for the federal government. I wrote press releases, reports, and speeches for federal officials who were in charge of helping people try to put their lives back together after major disasters.

What did you learn from these experiences?

Well, the first thing you learn is that everybody expects disasters to happen to *other* people. In fact, one of the early reviews of *Homesick* criticized the tornado scene as being unbelievable. But that's the thing about tornadoes: They *are* unbelievable. It's hard to comprehend the fact that everything you own can be destroyed in a matter of seconds. But here's something else you learn very quickly when you're in a disaster area: The worst things imaginable often bring out the best in people. I've never seen more generosity or kindness or profound wisdom than in communities that have suffered a major disaster.

What was your visit to Joplin like after the tornado?

Eerie. Quiet. It was summer, but the trees were all stripped bare of leaves. They looked like witches' fingers.

What kind of research did you do on hoarders while working on *Homesick*?

My editor, Liz Szabla, sent me several books to read about hoarding, which were fascinating. But most of my research came from talking to people. I realized everyone knows someone—or someone who knows someone—who has a really hard time throwing things away. We all have so much stuff in our basements, attics, and garages. Millions of people in this country can't park a car in their garage because it's filled with junk. Even more interesting to me is all the mental and emotional junk we hang on to. That's something I really wanted to explore in this novel.

Music is obviously an important part of Myron's life. Has music been important in your life, and if so, who are your favorite artists?

I write books, but I wish I could write songs. I really think music is the highest art. My life changed when I discovered Joni Mitchell and Laura Nyro. I also love Neil Young, Nick Drake, Jimmy Webb, and Stephen Sondheim. And of course, like Myron, I think Pete Townshend is a genius.

Are beignets your favorite pastry? What gave you the idea to name Benny after a deep-fried donut?

I started with his mother's name, Nola, which stands for New Orleans, Louisiana (NOLA). When I was in high school, I worked as a waitress with a woman from New Orleans named Nola. This is the kind of thing you don't think about for twenty or thirty years, but it's right there waiting for you when you sit down to write. Everyone in New Orleans loves beignets, so I thought that would be a perfectly appropriate—and awful—name for Nola to give her son. (And no, deep-fried donuts aren't really my cup of tea. I'd rather have a scone.)

What do you want readers to think about after reading *Homesick*?

Just that life is hard. There's so much bad stuff out there, from divorce to disasters to long bus rides with annoying classmates. But there's a lot of really good stuff, too, and good people. And that's what you have to cling to when the going gets rough.

What's the best advice you ever received about writing?

It's a quote from the French novelist Colette: "Sit down and put down everything that comes into your head and then you're a writer. But an author is one who can judge his own stuff's worth, without pity, and destroy most of it."

What's the best advice you ever received about life?

I often think of Albert Einstein's famous saying: "There are only two ways to live your life. One is as though nothing is a miracle. The other is as though everything is a miracle." I prefer to live the second way if only because it makes life more interesting.

After her brother, sister, and father die in a plane crash, Daralynn Oakland receives 237 dolls from well-wishers, resulting in her new nickname: Dolly. But she doesn't even like dolls! And when her mother's new job as a hairstylist at the local funeral home is threatened by the new crematorium, Dolly decides it's time to take action.

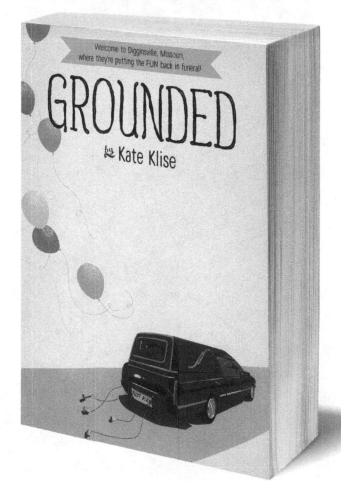

Keep reading for a sneak peek of

GROUNDED

ONE

Grounded in Digginsville

I'M ALIVE TODAY because I was grounded. Maybe that sounds odd to you, but it's true.

I was grounded by Mother for going fishing at Doc Lake without her permission. That's the only reason I wasn't in Daddy's plane when it crashed and killed him, my brother, and my little sister.

I was home sulking on the front porch, mad that I couldn't go flying with the others. Mother was inside, ironing in the kitchen and listening to "Swap Line." That was the name of a radio program. For five minutes every hour on the hour, folks would call in to the radio station and try to swap something they had for something somebody else had.

My mother loved "Swap Line." Nothing entertained her more than hearing people describe the junk they had in their basements and attics. For a woman who kept her house neat as a pin, listening to "Swap Line" was like listening to people confess their sins. Mother kept the kitchen radio turned on all day long so she wouldn't miss it.

Even from the front porch, I could hear her through the screen door, talking to the radio while she ironed.

"Bud Mosley, you've been trying to swap that cracked aquarium for three *weeks*," Mother said, howling with delight.

My mother knew everyone who called in to "Swap Line." She even knew their junk. In bigger cities, folks had news to listen to every hour. We had "Swap Line."

"Daralynn!" she called to me from the kitchen. "Come and listen to 'Swap Line.' It's a good one."

"I don't want to listen!" I hollered from the porch.

Truth was, I *did* want to listen. I was as hooked on "Swap Line" as anyone. But I suppose on that Sunday afternoon in late October I wanted to pout more.

I was kicking leaves in the yard when the state trooper's car pulled up in front of our house. It was

Jimmy Chuck Walters. He's the one who told us about the engine failing on Daddy's plane.

He told us in the kitchen. When he finished, Mother didn't cry. She just closed the front door, turned off the iron, and called Mamaw, my grandmother, who lived next door.

Right away, they started planning the funeral: *One service or three? Granite gravestone or marble? A reception at church or at the house?*

I wasn't much help in making the funeral arrangements. My brain couldn't take in all the information. It was like an old tree you can't fully see by just standing in front of it. You have to step around it slowly to understand how big it really is.

The world had changed. That much I knew.

But I confess the first thing I thought after I heard about the crash was: *I'd swap Bud Mosley a cracked aquarium for this.*

My second thought was: *If I'm the only kid left in my family, I bet Mother won't ground me as much anymore. I bet I won't get grounded again for the rest of my life.*

TWO

Hello, Dolly

Y OU WOULDN'T BELIEVE ALL THE DOLLS I got after
that.

For days, people drove up our driveway. Usually
they'd leave their cars running while they knocked
on the front door.

"I'm so sorry, honey." That's what most folks said
when I opened the door. Then they'd hand me a
doll.

Others whispered: "We're praying for you." And
then they'd hand me a doll.

Cloth dolls. Plastic dolls. Creepy baby dolls with
giant pink faces. Curvaceous Barbies. Barbie knock-
offs. Beautiful Crissy dolls with glossy red hair just
asking to be pulled.

I was buried alive in dolls.

And unlike the crockpots filled with ham and beans that arrived with the owners' names written on masking tape, the dolls weren't meant to be returned. They were for me. To keep.

One day Miss Avis Brown from *The Digginsville Daily Quill* came to the house. She wrote a story about me and all the dang dolls I was getting. It ran on the front page under the headline:

Hello, Dolly!
12-Year-Old Girl Receives 237 Dolls
After Family Tragedy

That's when a lot of people in town started calling me Dolly instead of my real name, which is Daralynn Oakland.

What everyone forgot was that *I* wasn't the one who *liked* dolls. That was my little sister, Lilac Rose. She was Mother's favorite.

Lilac Rose was named after the flowers Daddy gave Mother on their first date. Just like her name, Lilac Rose was pretty and prickly, especially when Mother brushed her hair.

Even at the funeral home, Mother spent hours bossing Lilac Rose's golden hair into perfect banana curls as she lay stretched out in her casket. Nearly every bone in Lilac Rose's body was broken, but she sure looked pretty. That was important to Mother.

Lilac Rose was nine years old when she died.

Wayne Junior was sixteen. He was Daddy's favorite. My brother wanted to be a pilot for Ozark Air Lines, just like Daddy. He probably could've done it, too. Wayne Junior was smart and good at math. But he wasn't as handsome as Daddy.

My daddy was the most handsome man in Digginsville. Every lady in town admired his blue eyes and sandy-blond hair. Even the girls in my class used to say he was more handsome than Paul Newman and Robert Redford combined, which filled me with pride and embarrassment, combined.

I didn't inherit good looks from my parents. With my brown ponytail and hazel eyes, I looked more like Daddy's sister, Aunt Josie, only without her makeup and dyed red hair.

It was a rare occasion to see Aunt Josie without her Passion Red lipstick and drawn-on eyebrows. In fact, the first time I ever saw Aunt Josie without her makeup was the day of the crash. She burst through our front door without even knocking.

"I just heard the news from Jimmy Chuck Walters!" Aunt Josie wailed. "It can't be true! Oh, Hattie, is it true?"

"It's true, all right," Mother said stonily.

That made Aunt Josie cry harder. "Those beautiful children," she moaned, collapsing in our front hallway. "Lilac Rose. Wayne Junior. And my sweet baby brother!"

Mother just stood there with her hands on her bony hips, staring straight ahead.

"How can it *be*?" Aunt Josie continued. "Oh my God in heaven above!"

Mother snapped. "Don't make a show of it, Josie," she directed. And then she walked upstairs and started picking out clothes for Lilac Rose, Wayne Junior, and Daddy to wear in their caskets.

I might not have been Mother's favorite, but I wasn't in last place. That distinction was held by Aunt Josie, who'd been at the bottom of Mother's list for as long as I could remember.

Aunt Josie's crying that day of the crash—the messiness of it all, the display of uncontrolled emotions, the fact that Aunt Josie wasn't even wearing lipstick—was contrary to everything my mother stood for. All she could do was wait for Aunt Josie to be on her way.

Looking back, I know Mother felt sad. I'm sure of it. But it's almost like she didn't know how to *do* sad. Not like Aunt Josie did, anyway. Crying wasn't Mother's style, just like wearing slacks wasn't her style.

So instead of getting sad, Mother got mad. A week after the crash, she paid Marvin Kinser from the hardware store thirty dollars to put a lock on her bedroom door. For almost nine months after the crash, I could hear Mother in her room, pacing the hardwood floor and slamming things down hard on her marble-top dresser. That's how mad she was.

At first, I hollered up to her whenever I heard "Swap Line" come on the kitchen radio. I knew she couldn't hear it upstairs. Mother didn't believe in keeping a radio or television in the bedroom. So I'd yell up the stairs: "Swaaaaaap Liiiiiiiine's on! You're gonna miss 'Swap Line.'"

Before the crash, Mother always wanted to know when it was on. That's why I kept hollering up to her. Sometimes I added, "It's a good one!" even though I couldn't hear what was being swapped.

I did that for weeks. I thought listening to her favorite radio show might cheer her up a little. But she never answered back. Somehow or other Mother had lost interest in hearing about the junk in other people's lives. Maybe because for once we had a fine mess of our own—and not a soul to swap it with.

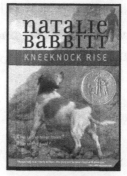